I0748489

EMILY ANDERSON

Bedtime Stories For Kids

Spend Wholesome Moments With Your Little One, Foster Their Imagination... And Ease Them Into A Magical Sleep Every Time!

Table of Content

Fairy and the Lost Wings 5
The Witness 13
Wolfy and a Toothache 17
Lucky Lucy 20
Christmas Apology 32
The Christmas Letter 34
The Toy Elf 37
Leaving Home for Christmas 40
Jimmy the Giraffe 43
Jayne the Jaguar Walks the Edge of the Jungle 46
The Monkey King 49
Elmo the Elephant is Very Happy 53
The Knowledgeable Bookworm 56
Life of Bailey 59
Vidal 64
Tilly the Turtle 68
Zane the Zebra 81
William's Adventures 96
The Butterfly Search and the Fairy 118
A First Plane Ride 147
Leonard and the Magical Carrot 150
Flying a Kite 154

Fairy and the Lost Wings

On the very edge of a forest, there grew an old oak tree. However, this was no ordinary tree. Aside from the chipmunks, birds, bugs, and beetles, it was home to extraordinary little beings. They had wings, yes, and their beds were oak leaves. They were called the fairies. With an average person's appearance, their size was that of a bumblebee, wearing clothes made of grass and flower petals and skirts made of shallow acorns. The fairies lived on the oak tree, having their little rooms carved in the bark.

They were spending their days waiting for the summer days, their favorite time of the year. Once the summer comes, they begin to go out of their homes, flying with butterflies and bees, enjoying themselves in the sweet juices of fruits and flowers. Fairies enjoy discovering new places and new green meadows in search of undiscovered plants and flowers. You shouldn't underestimate the fairies, as they love themselves a bit too much and tend to be harsh and impolite towards other living things in their surroundings. One such little fairy with a soft shirt made of rose petal and acorn skirt was minding her business one evening, preparing herself to sleep. She was exhausted because she spent the whole day collecting apple juice. She laid on her oak leaf bed, rest her head on her arms, and fell asleep.

The night passed, and the sun shone upon the oak tree. She felt sudden warmth on her body and yawned while stretching her arms. She sat up and rubbed her eyes. -What a beautiful morning! - She said and stood upon the leaf. -I could eat some pollen from that dandelion over there.

She thought and jumped in the air so she could fly to the flower. Suddenly and unexpectedly, she started soaring down the tree, falling fast. -What is happening? Where are my wings? - the fairy was yelling in fear while falling. She hit the giant wild rose that grew by the oak tree and landed on the ground. -I can't believe I don't have my wings! Who stole my wings! - she was so scared in disbelief of not knowing what happened to her wings. -I must find them! I can't live without them!

She stood up and cleaned her knees of dirt. After she stood there for a couple of minutes, she started thinking of a possible thief who took her wings. -Whom could it be? - she thought to herself. -I'm going to find out! –

The fairy walked to the little burrow in the tree trunk and entered through the small door made of tree bark. - Hello? Is anyone here? - she asked while going in. -Who is asking? What do you want? - little brown chipmunk was approaching the fairy. -I am looking for my wings. Have you seen them? - she asked and started searching through the room, turning the table and opening closets and drawers.

Uhm, they are not here. Could you stop doing that? It is not polite to get in someone's house and start to open things and make a mess. - the chipmunk was angry, waving his tail left and right. - Who cares what is polite? I want my wings! - she nodded her head and continued to make clutter. - You should leave before I call my friends, and they will not be as polite as I am! - the chipmunk started pushing the surprised fairy out of his house. She fell to the ground and was not aware of what she did wrong.

She continued her search and saw a giant bumblebee feasting on a freshly opened rosebud. -Hello! Did you steal my wings? Yours are quite similar to mine, so I bet those are my wings you're having! - she pointed towards the fat bumblebee. - I'm sorry, what? - he was flying above her and landed next to the fairy. -Did you call me a thief? Of your wings? Why would I wear fairy's wings? That's ridiculous! - he buzzed at her face and messed up her hair.

Yes, you did! You stole my wings! You thief, you robber! - the fairy started pulling his wings. - Give them back! - she pulled.

A dozen bumblebees were flying over them, overseeing this strange situation. They decided they should intervene and descended. - What's the trouble here? - asked the biggest one and stepped forward to the fairy. - She thinks I stole her wings and that I'm wearing them right now! - the hurt bum- blebee wrested from the fairy. He hid behind his friends.

You shouldn't go around making accusations if you're not sure, little one. That is a rude thing to do! - she was warned by one of the bumblebees. - Fine, have it your way! I don't care about being rude, and I want my wings back! - she turned her back on them and carried on. After a while, she felt drained and exhausted. She couldn't go up the tree and into her bed. She spent some time thinking about where to go and where to hide because soon enough, the sun will be gone, and the ground is no place to be on for a little, defenseless fairy. The only place she could think of was that chipmunk's house in the tree.

The night came soon, and the little fairy started to feel fear and insecurity. She ran to the door, and this time, instead of just breaking in, she knocked on the door and awaited the reply. - An old chipmunk opened the door and put on his reading glasses. - Yes? What do you want? -he asked bluntly when he recognized the fairy from before. - I'm- she stopped for a second. -I'm sorry for being rude to you sometime back. I know I should've asked for your permission to get in, and I apologize for being disrespectful to you. - she said quietly and leaned her head forward.

Now, that is a very polite thing to say! Saying that you're sorry can be hard sometimes, but it can only help you if you do. - replied the chipmunk and invited the humble fairy inside. - Can I, please, sleep here? As you've noticed, I can't find my wings and can't go up to my room. - she sat on a little wooden chair. - Sure, you can. You apologized, and I accept your apology. I will give you my bed, and I'll sleep on the floor. We can start finding your wings tomorrow morning. - said the chipmunk and made himself a little pillow out of moss.

The morning came, and both the fairy and the chipmunk were having breakfast. - Where do you think your wings could be?

He asked the fairy while eating acorn soup. -I don't know. - she frowned. After breakfast, they got out of the house. Fairy stretched her arms and saw the same bumblebee as the day before. She felt anxious and unhappy. -I've seen how you attacked that poor bug. He probably felt terrible and scared by you when you pulled his wings. It looked awful. - said the chipmunk and nodded his head in discontent. - I think you should apologize to him also. If you do so, you would feel better, and he would feel better as well. - the chipmunk halted. -You're right. I was wrong and attacked him for no reason, poor little creature. - the fairy agreed and walked towards the bumblebee.

Hey, you! Come down! - she yelled and waved her hand. The bumblebee recognized the fairy and was very reluctant to trust her, but he came down nevertheless. - I want to apologize to you and tell you I'm sorry for attacking you. You must have felt horrible!

I'm sorry for hurting you! - she cried. -Uh, well, that's okay. Thank you for saying sorry. It means a lot to me. - the bumblebee buzzed in joy and hugged the crying fairy. -You must feel very sad for not knowing where your wings are. I can help you find them! - he said and whistled to his flying friends. Soon, there was a swarm of bugs flying over them. - This little fairy apologized to me and asked if we can help her search for her wings! Go and pass over this oak tree and around it to see if her wings are stuck somewhere! - said the bumblebee and started to search as well.

The day was slowly passing by, and the fairy was jumping all around in the hope of finding her wings. She searched under the grass leaves, between the dandelions and daisies, and among the fallen oak leaves. The chipmunk was also running everywhere, climbing on the big oak tree, investigating the branches, and questioning other fairies who weren't rude and were willing to talk. Out of a sudden, a loud yell was heard across the meadow. - They're here! Your wings are here! - the bumblebee was buzzing around and came down in a hurry carrying fairy's wings. She jumped out of joy in the air and laughed loudly.

I can't believe it! My wings! Where did you find them? - she took them from the bumblebee and put them on. - They were underneath that oak leaf over there! - he was pointing towards the place where her room was located. - You mean you found them underneath my bed? Nobody stole them, but I lost them? - she was surprised and ashamed at the same time. I think you should thank this bug and all the other bumblebees who helped you find them! It is a nice thing to do.

Say, thank you. - whispered the chipmunk to the fairy's ear. - Thank you so much, she said, - I wouldn't have my wings without you helping me! And thank you, mister chipmunk, for allowing me to sleep at your place and for helping me too. - she felt grateful and fulfilled. She learned many things while her wings were missing. Being rude and impolite doesn't help you at all.

Nobody likes people who are disrespectful to others and having bad manners rejects everyone around you. Saying I'm sorry is hard, but if you use it when you're guilty, it opens up every door. The little fairy learned that respecting others' efforts, saying thank you is an encouraging thing.

By thanking others for their help and support, she made a lot of new friends. Even though she was rude to the chipmunk and bumblebee, once she apologized to them, they forgave her and even volunteered to help her find her wings. -I'm happy. I learned so much from you – concluded the fairy while flying next to the old chipmunk - I'll thank everyone for anything and apologize for anything I make or think wrong. I feel so much better when I know people are happy to be my friends! -she blinked at the chipmunk and flew up to her oak leaf. She laid on it, folded her precious wings, and closed her eyes. The day was over, and so was the search for her missing wings.

The Witness

There lived a man named Harry in some village. He was a wealthy man. He used to lend money to his villagers and help them from time to time, And the villagers used to return his money after harvesting and to sell their crops. Harry was a benevolent person, and so he never charged the villagers more than what he lent. He didn't believe in lending money on interest.

One-day Harry left his home for some other village. He had hardly gone out of his town when he happened to meet a man whose name was Tony. Tony saluted him and said humbly, "Seth Ji! My hut has become old and is in terrible condition. I want to have it thatched before it starts raining. Because if I don't get it thatched, the old thatched roof won't be able to bear the lashes of the rain. It would be so very kind of you if you could kindly lend me two hundred rupees for this purpose. I shall return your money with interest after selling my crops."

Harry pitied Tony and gave him two hundred rupees, But Tony did not stick to his promise. Though his crops had ripened and been harvested, and the next crop was about to be harvested, he did not even think of returning Harry's money. One day Harry called him to his residence and said to him with affection, "Tony! You have not yet returned my money. One year has already elapsed, and the second year also is coming to an end." "What are you talking about! I had borrowed money from you! No, sir! I have never borrowed money from you," said Tony exhibiting a little surprise.

Harry said, "Friend! Please try to remember. You had met me when l was on the way to some other village. You told me that you needed two hundred rupees to have your hut thatched. And seeing you in so sad a condition, I had lent you two hundred rupees. Now you are playing innocent as if you don't remember anything." "All right! Even if I have forgotten, you must be having the papers with my signature. Send the papers to me, and l shall pay you back the amount the papers show," said Tony. He knew it only too well that he had not signed any papers while borrowing the money from Harry. Harry said, "But I did not get any papers signed by you in return because I trusted you." "Harry Ji! I admit that you are a rich man and belong to a wealthy family.

But why is it that you are loading an innocent person like me with the burden of your debt," said Tony in a harsh tone. Seeing them arguing thus, some villagers gathered there. They asked them, "What is the matter! Why are you two quarrelling?" Harry explained to them everything in detail. But Tony declared him a liar, saying that he had not borrowed any money from him. He also noted that Harry took advantage of his status and was trying to extract money from him.

At last, the villagers suggested to them-" This problem can be sorted out with the chief of the village only. So let us all go to him." Tony said, "I am not afraid. I am ready to go to the chief of the village also." Thus all the villagers, including Harry and Tony, went to the chief of the village.

The chief of the village was very wise and intelligent. He listened to the arguments of Harry and Tony quietly. When asked for an explanation, Tony growled, "I am not a beggar. Why do I need to borrow two hundred rupees from him? I had had my hut repaired with the money I earned from selling my crops. If Harry had lent me money, why did he keep silent for such a long time? Why did he not get the papers signed by me during the last two years?" "Brother! There was none present when I gave you money. I had given you money under a banyan tree," said Harry.

The chief of the village said, "All right! We shall make the banyan tree our witness. Go and tell that tree that l have called it here." "What are you saying, chief? How can a banyan tree come here to appear as a witness?" asked Harry doubtfully. The chief said, "The banyan tree is bound to come once it comes to know that l have called it." Harry set off to convey the message to the banyan tree. Everyone around was astonished to hear the chief speak in this manner. Tony was pleased. He began thinking, "This old chief seems to have gone mad. How can a banyan tree stand witness to my borrowing money from Harry?" After observing silence for quite some time, the chief asked Tony,

"Tony! What do you think, would Harry have reached the banyan tree by now?"

Tony said, "How can he reach there so soon. That banyan tree is at a distance of four miles from here. Apart from the long-distance, it has also rained today. There is a pond in the way, and the road also must have become muddy due to rain. Then, there are so many banyan trees, and it would not be easy for him to locate that particular banyan tree." After hearing this, the chief struck Tony with a thick staff on his back and shouted, "You Swine! You are a thief! So you know under which banyan tree Harry had given you money." All the villagers were full of praise for the chief to see his wisdom. After a little more inquiry, Tony gave up and admitted that he had borrowed two hundred rupees from Harry two years ago. He had to return the money with interest.

Wolfy and a Toothache

Wolfy lived with his parents in Big Green Forest. He was growing up fast because he ate well: meat and vegetables, as well as fruit. But, even though he ate excellent and healthy food, Wolfy liked sweets the most. Candies, chocolates, bars, wafers, cakes, and ice creams: he loved them all. It was an excellent day for Wolfy: it was his birthday, and he had a fantastic birthday party. He invited a lot of friends and got a lot of sweets as presents. Even though he was a friendly wolf, Wolfy was selfish, so he decided to hide and eat all the sweets by himself. He ate dozens of candies, chocolates, and other sweets.

He was just about to open another bag of chocolate candies when he got a toothache.

"Ouch," cried Wolfy. "It hurts horribly! But I don't want to call my parents and ask for help! They will not be happy with my behavior. I will try to solve this toothache on my own."

Even though the toothache was getting worse, Wolfy decided to keep it a secret, as his parents surely would disapprove of his behavior. He didn't want to share the sweets, and he ate too many of them.

So, instead of getting some real help, Wolfy tried washing his mouth. At first, he rinsed with hot water. That didn't work. Then he tried rinsing with cold water, but that made the toothache even worse! He ran deep into the forest, so nobody could hear him cry. When Wolfy thought he was far enough, he started to cry loudly. An old owl resting high up in a tree heard his shrieks.

"What's the matter, Wolfy? I thought you had a nice birthday party today. Why are you crying so loudly?" asked the old owl. "Yes, I had a lovely birthday party earlier today. And I got a lot of nice presents, mostly sweets. I overate of them, and now I have a terrible toothache," replied Wolfy sadly. "Do you have a medicine for toothache, maybe?"

"Oh," said the old owl. "That's sad. I don't have a solution to your problem. You should go and tell your parents – they will surely take you to the dentist and the dentist will solve your problem fast."

"No! Not the dentist!" cried Wolfy.

“Wolfy, you shouldn’t be afraid of the dentist. He will help you,” replied the old owl.

Wolfy was ashamed because he was afraid of the dentist, so he lied to the old owl. “I am not afraid of the dentist. It’s just that my toothache is... gone,” said Wolfy and went more in-depth in the wood.

The toothache was getting worse, and Wolfy felt sorry that he didn’t wash his teeth more often. Suddenly, he got an idea to chew some plants, clean his teeth, and perhaps stop the toothache. Just as he started picking herbs, a bee flew to his face and sat on his nose.

“Hey, Wolfy! Picking flowers and herbs is not very nice. Those make my food,” said the bee.

“I am sorry, bee. It’s just that I have this terrible toothache, and I wanted to cure it with these herbs,” apologized Wolfy.

“Wolfy, these herbs cannot cure your toothache. Go to your parents, and they will take you to the dentist. That is the best solution,” said the bee.

The toothache got even worse, and Wolfy got tired. He returned home and told his parents about his toothache, so they took him to the dentist. The dentist turned out to be very gentle and very lovely, so Wolfy stopped being afraid. He cured Wolfy’s tooth and made him promise not to eat many sweets and to wash his teeth regularly.

Lucky Lucy

Lucy was an ordinary orange tabby to the untrained observer. If you saw her just once for a second or so, she may seem like an average cat. Appearances can be deceiving, for Lucy was the world's luckiest cat. She was not very big.

Lucy did not jump very high. She could not run fast. It was hard to say why this cat was so lucky. No matter how bad the situation was, Lucy walked away unharmed because The Olsen family rescued her from a shelter.

Little Cindy Olsen loved the little cat so much she held Lucy in her arms for the entire first month. By the time the little girl put Lucy down, the cat felt wobbly; she couldn't walk around. Lucy was close to the stairs and could have been hurt.

She fell onto a Frisbee and slid down. Then she flew into the air and sailed into the living room. The lucky cat landed on the couch without a scratch. That was the kind of life that Lucy led. When things went wrong, she didn't just land on her feet; and she would always land in a very comfy seat. Holden was a Highland Terrier and the Olsen family dog. He loved little Lucy.

He had also been rescued from a shelter. He was much older than Lucy, and he would laugh, "One day, Lucy, your luck is going to run out."

Then one day, when everyone was outside, Lucy's favorite ball rolled across the street. Lucy ran out to get it. She thought it was fine. Nothing ever happened to her anyway. Then she heard Holden yell, and she turned around. Little Cindy was following Lucy onto the road, and there was a car coming quick.

Lucy ran to Cindy, and Holden knocked over a garbage can. Lucy pushed Cindy inside, and when the car hit them, they went for a ride. Rolling around and around, the cat and the girl saw their whole town start to twirl. They watched as the houses spun right on past. They almost slowed down, and then they came to a big hill. If they thought it was fast before, this was faster still.

Near the bottom of the hill was a skateboard park. The garbage can be rolled right in, and they have launched off a ramp. Then the very dizzy friends sailed through the air. Luckily Lucy was there, and her luck was still good.

They landed with a splash in a public pool. Holden and the Olsen's were running down the street. It was impossible to keep up with the fast-moving can as the Olsen parents scolded Cindy.

Holden barked at Lucy, "You can't just walk out into the street; you have to set example for Cindy. She is always going to want to do what you do, and not everybody is as lucky as you." Lucy felt terrible, and she knew Holden was right. Lucy and Cindy were fine, luckily. Lucy was careful from that day on. She never tried to push her luck again.

Moral: Always be careful when crossing the street, no matter how lucky you are.

Lucy looked just like any other orange tabby. Most of her hair was a light orange, with dark orange stripes running down her back. However, anyone who got to know Lucy could see precisely why everybody called her Lucky Lucy. Most cats land on their feet.

Lucy landed with her feet on a pillow. She was just that kind of lucky.

The Olsen family rescued Lucy a few months ago. Up until then, she had been living on the streets. Three-year-old Cindy Olsen just adored her little orange cat. Lucy could not have found a more loving home if she had been able to choose one herself. Even the family dog, a Highland Terrier named Holden, loved Lucy. The Olsen family had adopted Holden before little Cindy was born.

He had helped Lucy learn the rules of the house. He was always there to say, "Don't scratch the sofa," and "Don't bring that mouse inside." Holden even let Lucy sleep in his dog bed when she was scared at night. One day as Lucy was sitting on a branch in the tall oak tree in the Olsen's back- yard, she watched Holden heading through the grass with something interesting in his teeth.

Lucy stayed very quiet as she saw the dog go under the fence. Holden dropped the package in the alleyway and headed back under the wall. It had to be food. Lucy could not understand why Holden would take delicious food and leave it outside the fence? Lucy decided she was going to get the food back. "Holden has lost his mind," Lucy thought to herself as she climbed down out of the tree.

The young tabby crawled under the fence and saw the package. It was a brown paper bag, but inside there was an open can of meat. It was excellent food. Lucy could not believe that Holden would leave the good food outside. Lucy took a quick look down the alley. No one was around, and so she ran towards the food. "What do you think you're doing, pet!" A deep voice growled.

Lucy could feel the voice come over her, and she froze with fear. It was Oscar. He was an old black tomcat that lived in the alley. Lucy knew she was in trouble. She started to back away. "Oh, I hope you don't think it is gonna be that easy."

Oscar started to chase Lucy down the alley. Lucy was too far from the hole underneath the Olsen's fence, and she had to sprint down the path to get away from Oscar's swinging claws. Lucy ran toward a plank that was leaning against the neighbor's fence.

Lucy sat at the end of the plank. Oscar ran at Lucy and jumped. Lucy ducked down and kicked Oscar up into the air as he passed her. Oscar hit the top of the plank, launching Lucy back into the limbs of the tall oak tree. Oscar landed in Mrs. Vanderbilt's composter.

As Lucy climbed down from the tree, she saw Holden coming through the yard. "Did you go and take that food!" The terrier was very cross with Lucy. Lucy just looked down. "Those cats and dogs out there in the alley don't get fed every day like you and me," Holden explained, "We are very fortunate to have what we have." Lucy felt terrible, and she had never thought about it like that. From that day on, Lucy helped Holden take food to the alley cats.

Moral: Giving is a reward.

Lucy was, well, she was orange. Lucy looked as normal as a cat could. If you saw her on the street, you would say, "Look, there is a cat." Or not even say anything at all. If, however, you got to know her, you would see that Lucy was about the luckiest cat in the whole world. While most cats can stroll along the top of a wooden fence, Lucky Lucy held the world record for blind-folded, one-legged fence racing.

The Olsen family a couple of months ago had adopted Lucy. At first, Lucy was scared of the big red brick house. Now it was her home, and she loved it very much. Lucy especially loved the fireplace. She could spend all day curled up beside the crackling heat of the fire. Today Lucy was trying to figure out how the fires got started.

She had seen Mr. Olsen light the fire a bunch of times. Lucy thought she could do it. She pulled a match out of the box with her teeth. And she tried to strike it against the side of the matchbox. A spark flew off the box as the match head hit against the rough strip. “EwwwYeoow!” Lucy yelled as the spark hit her.

The match went flying from her mouth, and she lost track of it. “Are you okay little Kitty?” three-year-old Cindy Olsen asked as she rushed in to scoop up her cat. Lucy was fine, but she loved to be held, so she let Cindy carry her away. She did not see the match sitting on a pile of newspapers.

Lucy and Cindy rolled on the floor of Cindy’s room together.

Cindy was dragging a shoelace across the floor. Lucy loved shoelaces. Toy mice were always a disappointment to a cat that used to live on mice's steady diet. Lucy had never had shoelaces before. As she chased the shoelace back and forth across the floor, Lucy began to pick up a strange scent in the air. She recognized it right away.

Suddenly Lucy remembered the match. “Where had it gone to?” Lucy took off down the stairs. Cindy was worried that something was wrong with her cat and trailed along behind her. The pile of the newspaper was set ablaze beside the fireplace. Lucy watched the flames as they turned the blue paint on the living room walls black.

The flames were stretching further and further up the wall. Lucy ran to the window.

The orange tabby saw Holden and Mr. Olsen playing fetch. Lucy banged on the window. The Olsen family dog and Lucy’s best friend, Holden, saw Lucy and the smoke billowing up behind her. Holden grabbed the stick he was fetching in his mouth. When Mr. Olsen tried to take it, Holden used the post to pull Mr. Olsen into the house. Cindy’s father smelled the smoke right away and got the fire extinguisher from the basement. The fire was out in minutes. Cindy was so happy she told her Dad all about how her cat had saved the house. “I wonder how the fire started?” Holden asked Lucy. Lucy just shrugged.

Moral: Never play with matches.

There are orange tabby cats all over the world. If you tried to meet everyone, you would still not meet one as lucky as Lucy. To the untrained eye, she was ordinary. She was orange with slightly darker orange stripes on her back. She had normal ears and an average tail. However, from the minute Cindy Olsen saw those bright blue eyes, she knew that she had found the unique cat in the world. Up until that point, Lucy had been living on the streets.

The young cat had been taking care of herself. So when little Cindy wanted to pamper her little kitty, Lucy didn't mind. Lucy didn't mind the bows Cindy put in her hair.

She liked all of the baths. Most cats don't like water. Lucy didn't either, but it made Cindy happy, and that was good enough. Cindy loved to put her little kitty in the Olsen's old baby stroller. Cindy would push the stroller all over the yard. Lucy didn't mind the stroller.

It was the seatbelt that drove her crazy.

She would try to fight to get it off every time. Cindy would always say, "No, no, no, Lucy, that is not safe!" Lucy didn't know why Cindy was worried. Lucy was fortunate. One day as Cindy pushed her cat around the yard, the sound of chimes filled the air.

Cindy knew that song could only mean one thing, "Ice cream!" She shouted as she ran out to the front yard. Lucy was bouncing all over the place as they hurried out to meet the truck. Cindy pulled the stroller out onto the sidewalk and got in line behind some of the neighborhood kids.

Lucy decided that she had had enough stroller time for the day, and she started to kick at the seatbelt to get free. Lucy did not know that Cindy had let go of the stroller already. The stroller edged towards the hill. The Olsen's lived at the top of Cherry Hill just before the start of the descent down the mountain.

Lucy struggled, not realizing how close she was to the edge. Cindy got her ice cream and turned just in time to see her stroller start to pick up speed.

"Whoooooosh!" The pit of Lucy's stomach dropped. She was free of the seatbelt finally, but she was now pinned to the seat by the speed of the stroller heading downhill.

Cindy followed behind her cat, yelling, "Stop! Stop Lucy!" And Lucy was screaming too, "Meeeeeeoooooooww!" she scratched.

The stroller headed downhill until it hit a plank in the middle of the road that jammed the wheels. Lucy was thrown high into the air. Lucy saw people rushing out to watch her. Mrs. Vanderbilt had both her hands on her cheeks as she stared with her mouth open.

The whole Smith-Pelly family was sitting on their porch, saying, "Oooooh!" As they followed Lucy through the air.

"Squish!" Lucy's journey ended with a soft squish. She found herself in a pile of manure that Mr. Roberts had just had delivered for his garden. It was a very smooth and very stinky landing. But she was safe!

Moral: Always wear your seatbelt.

Most days, if you saw Lucy, you would say, "That is the most ordinary orange tabby that there ever has been." She was unremarkable in many ways. Everyone who knew Lucy knew that this was not true. She was the most remarkable cat in the world. The second that the Olsen family saw this orange tabby in the Cherry Hill Animal Shelter, they knew that she was the perfect cat for them.

If most days she looked this way, then today was not most days. Today Lucy was standing at the top of a ramp with a firecracker in each paw. She was on a skateboard. Lucy looked down the ramp and said, "Okay, get my blindfold." As Oliver the squirrel tied the bandana over her eyes, Lucy began to think about how this day had started. Lucy was out in the yard telling a bunch of squirrels about how lucky she was.

She told them about the time Oscar the cat had chased her and the time she landed in the manure. "I never get hurt." bragged Lucy. She was going into a very long story about how she saved the Olsen family home from a fire when Oscar the cat appeared at the top of the fence.

"So, you are pretty lucky," Oscar said slyly, "Can't get hurt." Lucy did not like the smile on Oscar's face. It was the kind of smile that gave you the creepy crawlies. “Well, I bet you couldn’t jump off this fence and land in that wheelbarrow!”

Oscar said in a taunting sort of way. Lucy looked at the squirrels; they all wanted to see her do it. “Come on, and I dare you,” Oscar said.

After she landed in the wheelbarrow, Lucy had thought that she was done. Oscar was upset, and he challenged her to another dare. All-day long, Lucy had been doing things that Oscar dared her to do.

Lucy skateboarded up the fence, she did a bicycle flip off a ramp, and she climbed her house to the roof. Every time she finished a dare, Oscar had something else for her to do. That was how Lucy found herself holding firecrackers at this exact moment about to go off down the ramp.

Lucy was blindfolded and didn’t notice her best friend Holden, the Highland Terrier, come up behind her. “Lucy!” Holden shouted, pulling off her, blindfold, “You can’t do this!” He knocked the firecrackers out of her hand and pulled her off of the ramp. “But Oscar will call me a chicken!” Lucy protested as Holden led her away.

“Well, then I will call him a donkey!” The Olsen family dog said without stopping. “You can’t just do things because of a dare. You are very lucky, but that is no reason to endanger yourself.” Lucy felt very warm inside.

It made her feel good to have someone who cared for her as Holden did. Lucy never let Oscar bother her again, she knew she was lucky, and she didn't have to prove it to anyone.

Moral: Don't worry about being called chicken. Saying no takes more bravery than giving in to peer pressure.

Christmas Apology

"You kicked it in!" Jimmy yelled at me as I started to put my arms down. The rest of my team was still celebrating, but they all started to skate over to see what was happening. It was the worst part of having our ice rink; there were no referees, so everyone tried to referee. I knew that I had kicked it in. I was going to say something. At least I was pretty sure I was going to. I just wanted to celebrate for a minute. It was terrific that the puck went in. I redirected the spinning disc in mid-air with my heel. I just wanted to enjoy the moment.

"I did not!" I snapped back at him, "The puck bounced off me." I was lying, but I felt like it was his fault. Jimmy was always pushing my buttons. We were neighbors, and I think we had just known each other for too long because every time we got together, we just fought over everything. Jimmy and I yelled at each other until we were tired of talking, so I walked in my skates to the front of the house and sat on the stoop.

"You look down," I looked up to see a man with a white beard checking our electrical meter. "Is something wrong?" I was a little freaked out, but something about this man put me at ease.

"I just got in a fight with a friend of mine," I started, and as I began to talk, I could feel tears coming out of my eyes. "It was my fault.

I lied about something, but I couldn't do anything else. He drives me crazy." I heard myself, and I knew it sounded terrible. Why did I need to lie? I couldn't tell the truth because of who was around me.

"You're probably right. It was your friend's fault that you lied." "He pushes my buttons." I tried to defend myself even though I knew I was wrong. It was happening all over again. I was feeling I pushed to protect myself.

"The truth is hard sometimes, but no matter who is with you, it is always the right course. You cannot let people change who you are as a person. I know you," the man smiled. I put my head down; I knew the man was right as he continued, "I mean, I think I know who you are, and I know that you will do the right thing." I looked up when he finished talking, but he wasn't there. I looked all around, but the older man had vanished.

I walked back around to the rink, apologizing to the guys about lying, and I even apologized to Jimmy. "I didn't see it," he admitted, "I just didn't want you to score." Jimmy turned red, but I put my hand on his shoulder and told him not to worry about it.

We both promised each other not to lie to or about each other anymore. As we shook on it, I saw a red streak appear across the sky.

The Christmas Letter

Dear Santa,

So, how is everybody treating you? I never know how to start letters. I was thinking of sending you an email, but Mom said that these sorts of things have to be handwritten. It also helps that she took away my laptop and my tablet, and I am banned from using the family computer until next week. I know you will hear all sorts of wild stories about me and talk of mischief, but I will set the record straight. I did it.

David pushed me first is my only defense. Yes, I was the one who super-glued his hand to his face, but he made me first. I know last year I promised to stop super gluing people to things after gluing

Dad's hand to the alarm clock, but this time I glued a person to himself, so it feels different. I know that I am the older brother and should be more responsible and whatever, but he is annoying.

I try, but I can only do so much. Brian is an entirely different story. He is a tattle-tale, and I cannot stand it. Mom and Dad tell him not to tattle, but they don't seem to mind being fed all the information. I need them to make up their minds on this one. Am I wrong for gluing people, or is he wrong for telling on me? I am only telling you this. I knew he was in the closet when I locked the door and blocked him in.

I didn't mean to leave him there for so long, but there was a Mighty Men marathon on TV. I know Mom has already said that I won't be getting anything for Christmas this year, and she is probably right. I just wanted to ask you for a couple of things. Brian wants to get that action figure, I know he put a lot of stuff on his list, but the most important thing was the Mighty Men action figure.

David needs a new hockey stick and a better helmet; he hates having to use my hand-me-downs. As for me, I don't need anything. I have every toy and gadget I could ever want. I will just ask for more patience, and I do want to be a good big brother.

I keep getting myself in trouble, and I am tired of it. I hope I don't get any presents this year because I know I have been wrong and the rules are apparent on Christmas presents. I will try harder next year.

Thanks,

Jimmy Swanson

P.S. next year I want a bike. A blue one!

The Toy Elf

It was the same thing every year. The last-minute push to get toy orders in was right before Christmas, so many kids decided to be fair and try for a present. Gregory had been through this every Christmas for the last 200 Christmases.

As he saw the rush orders piling up, something snapped inside that caring little elf. "I am not going to make toys for anyone," he yelled, "They are all for myself!" The elf turned his chair away from his friends, and he started making toys for his toy room.

Gregory made trains and pop-guns, made yo-yos and teddy bears, and even made a remote-controlled car. He was putting them all into a wagon he had made to carry them home in. It felt good to make toys for himself for a change.

Gregory made the things that he had always wanted to have, but he had never had time to make them. When you are an elf, you can make any toy, but you are so busy that you rarely get to play with those toys. For the most part, elves don't mind because they like to do things for others. It makes them feel good. But Gregory was tired, and he wanted to play. Santa heard about what Gregory had said, and he decided to head down to the workshop. Santa saw Gregory sitting by himself with his pile of toys.

The jolly old elf sat down beside his young friend and asked him what was wrong, and Gregory explained what had happened to the elves on that day. "I know that it is hard to make toys all the time," Santa said to his friend. "I have an important job for you to do that might help slow down the number of toy orders coming through."

Santa led Gregory to the List Double-Checker, a big glass ball that helped Santa do his job. "Look through the updated list and find me the children that have not done enough good." Santa handed the list to Gregory, "Mark their names off, and then we won't have to make them toys." Gregory was so excited about his new job. It made him feel important. He put the list in a slot that said "in here," The machine fired up and started showing Gregory pictures.

The images were of young Bobby Larue on the naughty list because he yelled at his mother. As Gregory watched Bobby clean up around the house, he was superior to his brothers and his father too. Then Gregory watched Cindy Himelfarb, who was naughty this year because of a pie-making incident.

She had since apologized and behaved very well. It seemed like all the kids acted very well, and though Gregory wanted to, he couldn't take their toys away. Santa walked Gregory back to the workshop, and together they wheeled all the toys he had made to space under the tree. Gregory knew that he needed to share these toys with all of these amazing girls and boys.

Leaving Home for Christmas

The park Christmas tree is 60 feet tall. I love just to watch it glow. I have always come to see this tree with my family, and it is one thing that always calms me down and puts me in a better mood. It is something about the lights or maybe the sounds. Everybody talks in a happier tone around the tree. I grabbed a seat on the bench and stared at the tree; it felt like the right place to be. It had all started a couple of hours ago. My sister Kim got me into a bunch of trouble. I didn't do anything, and so, of course, my parents took her side, and I was in a colossal problem while nothing happened to her. She was the one who started arguing with me.

I was watching TV, and she came in and changed the channel. Kim is two years younger than I am, and she is always getting her way. My parents are wrapped around her sticky, devious fingers.

I had decided earlier this month to cut off all contact with her until after Christmas. I was just done fighting and getting in trouble over the problems that she started. I stared at the beautiful tree, and I let my problems melt away. It was getting a little chilly, and it had started to snow, but I could not go home; there was just no way to live in that house and not fight with Kim. I heard some carollers coming down the road.

They were singing, "Oh Holy Night." It had always been one of my favorite songs. I watched as they approached the tree, and I just drank in their music. I didn't even notice that he had sat down beside me. "So you just leave without asking now?" My Dad said as I sat back down, "How long have you been out here."

"Just a little while," I lied as I started to feel a shiver come up my spine. I tried to think of more words to say, but they just wouldn't come. I wanted to tell him how mean Kim was being and how she always got me in trouble. I tried, but I couldn't say anything. I just felt like I was going to cry.

"I know she gets you are going," Dad said as I still tried to find words, "She is in trouble too, we turned the TV off, and nobody can watch it right now. But TV is no reason to run away."

"I am not running away." I cried, "I am just staying here until after Christmas so that I can be on the nice list." That was the truth. I just felt like I needed to be away from her.

"Kim is devastated right now," Dad said, "She went to apologize to you, and you were not in your room." Dad put his arm around me as I shook.

"You just need to relax and not let her get to you. You can't stay out here until Christmas. It is too cold. What you need to do is figure out how life with your sister. She loves you, and you love her."

Dad and I sat under the tree for a while longer, and then we went home. I hugged my sister. She was still crying about driving me out of the house. It made me feel good to know that she loved me, and remembering helped me stay calm when she got back to being herself the next day.

It was breakfast, she turned off my show and put on some rainbow pony show, and I smiled and hugged her. TV is fun, but it is not as important as my little sister.

Jimmy the Giraffe

Jimmy, the giraffe, is a very cute and adorable giraffe who likes to help out the other animals in the jungle. Jimmy was sitting underneath his favorite tall tree when he decided that he wanted all the animals in the wilderness to get along and be friends.

“How can I be friends with all the animals?” asked Jimmy to his best friend, Jayne the jaguar.

“Well,” said Jayne. “I am not sure that you are going to be able to be friends with all the animals in the jungle, but there is no harm in trying.”

Jimmy thought about what Jayne had said. “You and I are best friends,” said Jimmy. “Whoever would have thought that a jaguar and a giraffe could be the best of friends?" "I suppose you are right," said Jayne.

"I guess it is a little odd that we are best friends since we are so different." "But," said Jimmy.

"I think it is our differences that bring us so close to each other." "Very true," said Jayne. The next morning, Jayne came along while Jimmy was eating from his favorite tall tree.

"I am so hungry," said Jayne. "So are all the rest of the animals in the jungle. I sure wish I could reach high up in the tree as you can."

"I can help you," said Jimmy. "I see some very ripe fruit way up here. I can pick them and give them to you."

Jayne was very grateful for the fruit that Jimmy was able to get for her. Soon, several of the other animals in the jungle were seeking Jimmy's help for food. Jimmy felt very important that the other animals relied on him to feed them.

"I feel fragile today," said Jimmy, confiding to Jayne. "It is no wonder," said Jayne. "Here you are feeding everyone else, and you are not eating much yourself. It would help if you started looking after yourself first and then feed us. We need you to be strong and healthy for us."

Jimmy decided that what he would do was feed himself first and then help the others with food once he had eaten. He found that by taking care of himself first, he became stronger and healthier and could take care of the others.

"Come here, Jimmy," said Jayne near the end of the hot season in the jungle. "What do you want?" asked Jimmy, confused. "Just follow me," said Jayne.

Jimmy followed Jayne. She led him to an opening in the jungle, and all the jungle animals were gathered there.

"This is a special celebration just for you," said Jayne. "This is to show you that we appreciate what you have done for us."

"Oh, dear," said Jimmy. "How can we celebrate without food? I must go get us some food." "We have everything arranged," said Jayne. "This is your day, and we are going to feed you. You have to relax."

Jimmy thought it was very kind of the jungle animals to hold this special celebration for him. He sat back, relaxed for the rest of the day, and enjoyed his celebration.

Jayne the Jaguar Walks the Edge of the Jungle

Jimmy, the giraffe, was standing underneath his favorite tall tree in the jungle. He had just finished eating and was very content. He was just about to doze off for a nap.

“Hi Jimmy,” said Jayne, walking by him.

“Hi Jayne,” said Jimmy, yawning.

“I am glad to see you,” said Jayne.

“I’m glad to see you too,” said Jimmy.

"Good," said Jayne. "I am glad to hear that because I need your help."

"What do you need my help with?" asked Jimmy.

"Well," said Jayne. "I think it is time we take a walk to the edge of the jungle and find out what is there."

"Oh," said Jimmy. "Why do we need to walk to the edge of the jungle?"

"Aren't you curious about what is out there?" asked Jayne.

"I am," said Jimmy. "But I am also scared at what we may find."

"I am scared too," said Jayne.

Jimmy wasn't sure, so he thought about it for a while.

"I do agree with Jayne," said Jimmy. "I do think it is time we found out what is at the edge of the jungle."

All the jungle friends decided that they would take a walk together to the jungle's edge and see what they could see.

"Oh my!" exclaimed Jimmy, as they got closer to the edge. "All I see is sand."

"Then it hasn't changed at all," said Jayne. "My Uncle Peter had told me the last time he was at the edge of the jungle that it was all sand."

"Wait," said Jimmy, standing on the highest hill of sand he could find.

“What do you see?” asked Jayne.

“There is a beautiful city about 10 miles from here,” said Jimmy. “There are buildings made of steel and glass, and there are a ton of people walking around the city streets.”

“Do you think we should visit the city?” asked Jayne.

“You know,” said Jimmy. “I think the people in the city know that our jungle exists because there is a distinct gap between the jungle and the city. I think they respect the fact that the jungle is here.”

“I think Jimmy is right,” said Jayne. “I think we should respect the people and leave them to be as they have done to us.”

The jungle animals turned around and walked back into the jungle. They never left the jungle to bother the people in the city, and the people in the town never bothered them. They lived in peace and harmony with each other.

The Monkey King

Jimmy, the giraffe, was in the jungle hanging out with the rest of his jungle friends. They were all too excited and delighted. They were all anxiously waiting for the birth of their new king, a baby monkey.

"It has been a long time since we have had a new king born in the jungle," said Jimmy excitedly. "I am so happy!"

"Oh, me too!" exclaimed Jimmy's best friend, Jayne the jaguar. "I am very excited, as well. Look at my tail! It won't stop wagging!"

Jimmy was the tallest animal in the jungle, so the other animals wanted him to be their lookout.

"Jimmy," said Jayne. "You should go find the tallest hill in the jungle and stand on it and see if you can see anything!"

"Good idea," said Jimmy.

Jimmy found a tall hill, and within minutes, he was standing on top of it, looking all around him.

"Do you see anything?" the other animals kept asking him.

"No," said Jimmy, turning his head in every direction. "I don't see anything yet."

"Let us know when you do," said Jayne.

"Yes," said Jimmy, and then a few minutes later, he exclaimed. "Oh my!"

"What do you see?" asked Jayne, not able to contain her excitement. "What do you see?"

"I see a tiny baby monkey," said Jimmy.

"Then the king is born!" exclaimed Jayne. "I am so excited!"

"Who saw the baby king first?" the current king exclaimed, coming down to greet the crowd of jungle animals.

"Jimmy, the giraffe, was the first one that saw the baby king," said Jayne, proudly.

"Jimmy," said the king, outstretching his paw toward Jimmy. "I declare you the best friend of the newborn king!"

The jungle animals all applauded Jimmy and cheered him. Jimmy felt like he was on top of the world. He was very honored to be the best friend of the new baby king.

"You know," said Jayne. "The one who sees the baby king first is considered very lucky."

"I guess I am fortunate then," said Jimmy, happily.

"Yes," said Jayne. "You are fortunate!"

Jimmy took a little walk, and on his walk, he found a fresh pool of water.

"Oh, dear!" exclaimed Jayne. "You are lucky! We have all been looking for some freshwater for a few days now."

"I guess I am fortunate," said Jimmy. "And all because I saw the new baby king first."

Later that day, Jimmy found a new grove of bananas.

"Oh my!" exclaimed Jayne. "You found a new grove of bananas. That is so lucky!

You will be able to take some to the new baby king."

Jimmy took many fresh bananas to the new baby king, and the baby king ate them all up.

"You are fortunate," said the baby king's father. "We have been trying to get him to eat, and you are the only one he would eat for."

Jimmy kept being lucky, and he knew it was all because he had been the first to see the new baby king.

Elmo the Elephant is Very Happy

Jimmy, the giraffe, was eating from his favorite tall tree in the jungle when he heard a thundering crash from the jungle's eastern section.

“What was that noise?” asked Jimmy’s best friend, Jayne the jaguar.

“I am not sure, “said Jayne. Jimmy and Jayne looked over to the east, in the direction the noise was coming from. They were very excited to see an elephant standing in the clearing.

“An elephant!” exclaimed Jimmy. “I can’t believe an elephant is revisiting our jungle!”

"It sure has been a long time since we have seen one," said Jayne.

Jimmy went up to the elephant. He wanted to be friends with the newcomer.

"Hi," said Jimmy.

"I am Jimmy, the giraffe, and this is my best friend, Jayne, the jaguar."

"Hi, Jimmy," said the elephant.

"My name is Elmo the elephant."

"What are you doing in our part of the jungle?" asked Jayne.

"I wanted to find some freshwater to drink," said Elmo.

"In the part of the jungle that I live in, we don't have any freshwater left."

"Oh, dear," said Jimmy. "We can share our fresh water with you.

We have tons of it." "That would be wonderful," said Elmo.

Jimmy and Jayne took Elmo to their freshwater supply, and Elmo took a long drink. Elmo was delighted that he was able to have a drink.

"Thank you so much," said Elmo.

"That was very refreshing."

"You are very welcome," said Jimmy.

“Well,” said Elmo. “I think I have to go back to my part of the jungle now.”

“Do you have to go back?” asked Jimmy. “Why can’t you stay here?”

“I guess I could stay here,” said Elmo. “I don’t have anything in my part of the jungle.” “We would like to have an elephant living in our part of the jungle again,” said Jayne. “We love elephants.”

“Okay,” said Elmo. “Then, I will stay.”

Elmo was pleased that he was able to stay. He made many new friends. All of the animals in the jungle noticed that Elmo was always delighted. “How could he be happy all the time?” Jimmy asked Jayne one day.

“Well,” said Jayne.

“I suppose if this part of the jungle was all dried up and we came across a part of the jungle that welcomed us in, I suppose we would be delighted as well.”

“Yes,” said Jimmy. “I do think that makes perfect sense.” Jimmy, Jayne, the other jungle animals, and Elmo found they were all delighted living in the jungle together. They all got along wonderfully and were all the best of friends.

The Knowledgeable Bookworm

It was a sweltering day in the jungle. Jimmy, the giraffe, was lying down in the cool tall grass.

"I think I need to get some fresh cool water," said Jimmy standing up.

"Where are you going to find some fresh water in this heat?" Jimmy heard a little voice ask. Jimmy looked over into the grass, and he saw a tiny worm speaking to him.

"I know of a place just over that knoll," said Jimmy, pointing straight ahead toward a knoll.

"I am afraid that water is all dried up," said the bookworm.

"How do you know that?" asked Jimmy curiously.

"I know everything," said the worm. "I am a knowledgeable bookworm. "Well," said Jimmy. "If you are knowledgeable, then where would you go to get water?" "You can go to the other side of that knoll," said the bookworm, pointing to the opposite direction in which Jimmy was going to go.

"I was there yesterday," said Jimmy. "There was no water there."

"It rained over there last night," said the bookworm. Jimmy went to where the worm had pointed out that there was water. Sure enough, there was plenty of fresh water there. Jimmy took a long drink, and he was very refreshed and very grateful for the knowledgeable worm.

Jimmy saw his best friend Jayne the jaguar. She was on her way back from the direction that Jimmy was going to go in the first place.

Jayne looked very thirsty. "I bet there was no water there," said Jimmy.

"You are right," said Jayne. "How did you know?"

"I met up with a knowledgeable bookworm this morning," said Jimmy. "Follow me, and I can show you where there is some water."

"Yes, please," said Jayne. Jayne followed Jimmy to where the water was, and she took a very long drink. She felt very refreshed. Jimmy talked to Jayne about the knowledgeable bookworm. "How come he knows everything?" asked Jimmy.

"He is very knowledgeable because all he does is read books and read newspapers," said Jayne. "I see," said Jimmy. "Why is that all he does?"

"Well," said Jayne. "A worm is a tiny creature. Therefore, they don't have to spend their whole day looking for food because they only eat minimally. It wouldn't take them long to eat.

Therefore, they have the rest of the day to do whatever they want to." "That would make sense," said Jimmy. "It will be nice to have a friend like the knowledgeable bookworm. Then we can ask him questions and get a knowledgeable answer."

"Yes," said Jayne. "That would be nice." The next time Jimmy saw the knowledgeable bookworm, he asked him if he wanted to be his friend.

"I would love to be your friend," said the knowledgeable bookworm. "I was wondering if you could do me a favor, though."

"What do you want?" asked Jimmy. "Well," said the knowledgeable bookworm. "I would like to know if you could lift me high into that tree. There is a yummy leaf there that I would like to eat."

"Absolutely," said Jimmy. Each day, Jimmy would lift the knowledgeable bookworm into the tall tree. He would give Jimmy any information that Jimmy wanted. The two became inseparable, and Jimmy found that he was becoming very knowledgeable as well.

Just for Fun Activity

Jimmy, the giraffe, is a very tall animal. He sees things differently than we do because he is looking down at something most of the time. Draw a picture of what your house or street would look like if you were a giraffe.

Life of Bailey

Bailey was born on a farm in the springtime. He was small and an unusual light brown color, with white paws and floppy ears. He was also very playful.

Bailey did everything with his brothers and sisters. They explored what was around them often, but most of all, Bailey liked to sleep and stay warm with them.

The day came when Bailey and his siblings needed homes of their own. One morning someone new came to take Bailey away. It was hard to say goodbye to his brothers and sisters, but his new human seemed very lovely.

Bailey's new Daddy took him into his arms and calmly whispered, "Hello, little one, I'm going to call you Bailey. I'm your new Daddy, and soon, you will meet your new Mommy. I know you are sad, but I promise to give you a wonderful life."

Bailey was afraid because everything started changing for him. Suddenly, his brothers and sisters were gone, and he had never been in the back seat of a car before.

It was a long and bumpy ride home. This was hard for Bailey because it made Bailey feel tired and lonely.

On the way home from the farm, Bailey's new Daddy stopped at an animal shelter to check that Bailey was healthy and met his new Mommy.

When Bailey arrived outside his new home, he was unsure about all the new smells and sounds of downtown Toronto. It was very different, and it made him nervous. Bailey met his new Mommy. She was happy to meet Bailey but noticed how unsure the puppy was.

There were loud sounds all-around from cars, airplanes, boats, and motorcycles. The air smelled different than on the farm, and there were people everywhere.

Later that evening, Bailey tried to sleep in his new bed for the first time. He couldn't relax, and he cried because he missed his old life on the farm.

As the days went on, Bailey began learning all kinds of things. Every day after playtime, Daddy taught Bailey to look at him, sit, stay, lay down, and come when called.

Bailey peed and pooped on the floor at home all the time, but Daddy didn't mind. Daddy just smiled and said, "That's okay, Bailey, we will do better next time."

Soon, Bailey and Daddy were busy learning all the time. He forgot about his old life on the farm, and Bailey was happy again.

Bailey liked to explore. Every day, Daddy took Bailey to a particular park by the lake to see the ducks, squirrels, fish, and horses. Daddy told Bailey he used to go to the very same park when he was a boy. It was a special place for both of them and made them happy. Bailey even learned to sit still so he could make friends with all the animals.

Bailey learned to explore his new home in the big city with Daddy safely. Sometimes Mommy came too. Bailey learned to walk with Daddy and Mommy slowly and to cross the street carefully.

Each day, there were many times, and Bailey practiced how to pee and poo outside when Daddy said, "Go potty." He was always glad to do good for Daddy.

Bailey kept learning so much from his daddy. Learning so much made him tired. So Bailey would nestle up on Daddy's lap and fall asleep. Then Daddy carried Bailey to his bed and said, "Goodnight Bailey, you're such a good boy."

As time went by, Bailey's Mommy had trouble breathing when Bailey was close to her. Daddy and Mommy weren't sure Bailey could stay. It made the sweet dog feel very bad.

Daddy called Bailey's new grandma and told her he was concerned. Grandma suggested Bailey stay with her for now. So Daddy took Bailey to Grandma's house. Bailey was confused that he had to leave and sad too.

Meanwhile, Daddy and Mommy had to decide whether to keep Bailey or give him away to another home. Mommy cried a lot, and Daddy hugged Mommy.

Daddy and Mommy saw a particular doctor about what to do next. They hoped the doctor could help.

Meanwhile, Grandma was practicing the things Daddy taught Bailey. She also taught Bailey how to be calm for bedtime.

Bailey still cried a lot because he missed Mommy, Daddy, and his home. What if he never saw them again? But Grandma was patient and kind to Bailey. She spoke softly and said, "Everything will be fine, Bailey. Put your head down and sleep now." And Bailey listened to Grandma.

Daddy came to visit Bailey at Grandma's house. Bailey was thrilled and jumping all over Daddy, licking his face and crying for joy. Daddy had to stay late at night at Grandma's house to keep Bailey calm. Daddy lay down beside Bailey, waiting for him to fall asleep, but Bailey would not sleep.

When Daddy had to leave to check on Mommy, Bailey cried. He felt lonely.

Mommy's particular doctor ordered more tests to help Mommy breathe better when she was around Bailey. But nothing helped.

Mommy did not give up. She spoke to her friends and an extraordinary nurse for advice. The advice helped, and soon Mommy felt better.

Daddy was still concerned, but he wanted everyone to be happy. He asked Mommy to try living with Bailey again. Mommy said, okay.

Daddy brought Bailey home from Grandma's house to see Mommy again. Bailey was happy and hugging Mommy, jumping, and licking Daddy and Mommy's faces.

Mommy was a little scared when Bailey came home. She wasn't sure she could live with Bailey because his fur made it hard for her to breathe. But little by little, Mommy's breathing got better, and her smiling face came back.

Daddy, Mommy, and Bailey celebrated being a family. Bailey finally felt he belonged with Daddy and Mommy forever.

Vidal

Once upon a time—in the day of dragons—there lived a shy man named Vidal.

He lived near the small town of Bodington in a hill which he had carved out himself with the help of spells. It was enormous inside and just right for his work. Not only did it blend into his surroundings, but it protected him from the worst weather. Although he had a reputation for caring for all sorts of wild creatures, only his cat, Blanchette, shared his abode.

No one in the town could say for sure how long Vidal had been in the area—may be twenty years, maybe more. He was a modest man who kept to himself most of the time. However, occasionally village folk would be reminded of his presence when a puff of pink smoke might be seen coming out of his chimney.

If he were reclusive, it was for a good reason. He was a wizard. In his youth, he had been an apprentice to one of the great- est wizards of that time—Ozwald. He had applied himself whole-heartedly to learning spells and contra-spells and had been successful. Still, his lack of showmanship soon had him relegated to more menial tasks. It was then that he decided to set out on his own and work his magic as needed and not as a means of entertaining people and earning money.

He certainly had no interest in casting spells for those who wanted to rise above their opponents or take revenge against them. From an early age, he had been interested in creating an in- visibility spell. Who as a child has not imagined being invisible? Having many parchments with ancient periods noted on them, he spent a great deal of time reading them in hopes of finding the right formula or incantation to make things invisible, perhaps, even himself.

Following the instructions for several spells, he developed a paste he hoped would make him invisible when he smoothed some on himself. He was disappointed that nothing happened. He added other ingredients making a light cream, still without success.

One of his scrolls was written that rainbows had seven colors. However, the seventh one, ultra-violet, was not visible to the naked eye.

That got him to thinking that perhaps he could extract ultra-violet from things around him. He began by making a syrup from blueberries that wouldn't be toxic to drink. Hopefully, the person drinking it (himself) would become invisible.

He spent a lot of time concocting the liquid in his workshop while stirring in a soft spell. The resulting cordial was a pleasure for the eyes. The taste was delightful, yet it did not make him invisible. Naturally, he would have been surprised to succeed on his first try, but other attempts with more potent spells changed nothing.

That got him to thinking that perhaps he could extract ultra-violet from things around him. He began by making a syrup from blueberries that wouldn't be toxic to drink. Hopefully, the person drinking it (himself) would become invisible. He spent a lot of time concocting the liquid in his workshop while stirring in a soft spell. The resulting cordial was a pleasure for the eyes. The taste was delightful, yet it did not make him invisible. Naturally, he would have been surprised to succeed on his first try, but other attempts with more potent spells changed nothing.

Once again, despite the number of spells he used, the resulting liquid did not make him invisible. He smelled quite strongly of those flowers he had picked. He continued with various other products and spells but failed every time.

The day arrived when he wanted to give up. He felt he was a failure. His cat, Blanchette, tried to console him, but he was lost in his unhappiness.

A couple of the villagers came to his dwelling because they hadn't seen him for a while. His neighbors hoped he wasn't ill. Seeing he was in the doldrums, one of the villagers came forward and asked what the problem was, thinking he might be able to help. When Vidal explained he'd failed the vital project he was working on, the neighbor spoke up.

"You may have failed with this job, but think of all those where you have succeeded. Grandma Brown can walk now without hobbling, thanks to that paste you gave her for her foot. Little Johnny Johnson's sores healed once he used your cream. The cordial you gave us was perfect when all the children in the village had coughs. It soothed their throats. And just think of all those women you have made happy with the violet scent.

Everyone loved those colored bubbles you made, too. They were so festive when we had the village fete."

He paused with a smile, seeing Vidal had cheered up with the memory of his successes with the villagers. Well, perhaps they weren't the accomplishments he'd intended, but they were well received and appreciated by everyone else. "Why, thank you for your kind words. I feel better already," he told the men. They all shook hands and said good-bye.

As Vidal entered his home with Blanchette, his thoughts were already planning his next spell with the shells.

Tilly the Turtle

Tilly the Turtle is the happiest turtle in the world. She is happy because all her worldly possessions are carried with her on her back. If she gets tired, she can just find a shady spot, put her head in her shell, and fall asleep.

"It is so nice outside today," said Tilly. "I think I want to go to the beach."

"I would go too," said Tilly's brother, Billy the Turtle. "However, look up at the sky. I think it is going to rain."

Tilly thought that what Billy had said was hilarious. She started laughing.

"Why are you laughing?" asked Billy. "We are turtles," said Tilly. "We love the water. Why would we care if it rains?"

"Oh," said Billy, thinking for a moment. "Yes, I suppose that is true. We do love water. However, I did just come back from the beach. I have been in the water all day, and I did want to dry off for a bit."

"Okay," said Tilly. "I can understand that."

Tilly walked over to the beach, and as soon as she got to the beach, it did start to pour rain. She let the raindrops fall onto her head. It was very refreshing to feel the cool drops of rain on her head. She was hot, and the rain was helping to cool her down.

Tilly was laughing as she walked on the beach. She was delighted. She loved being able to walk in the sand. She noticed, though, that she was getting a lot of sand in between her toes. She decided she would roll over on her back and point her toes straight up into the air. That way, she could let the rain clean off her toes.

"Oh my, that tickles!" exclaimed Tilly when the raindrops fell onto her toes.

Tilly laughed as each drop of rain hit her toes. When her toes were nice and clean, she rolled over and let the rain clean off her back.

"Oh, it feels so nice to be clean," said Tilly.

Tilly started to walk home, but then she noticed that it had rained so much that it had created a big river in the sand.

"Oh, dear!" exclaimed Tilly. "All my turtle friends are going to drown if it keeps flooding. What can I do to help them?"

Tilly thought for a moment, and she knew that she would be too late if she went for help. She knew she must do something right away.

"I will dig a hole at this end of that big river," said Tilly. "That way, I can see if I can divert some of the water away from the area my friends are in."

Tilly started digging in the sand. She dug a huge hole, and the faster she dug, the faster the water from the big river began to pour into it.

"Oh, good!" exclaimed Tilly. "What I am doing is working!"

"Tilly," said her brother, Billy, worried about her and came to find her. "What are you doing?"

"I am digging this hole to divert water away from our friends," said Tilly continuing to dig and not bothering to look up.

"I think you were able to save our friends," said Billy, going to check on the status of the river at the other end. "It is dry over where our friends are."

Tilly stopped her digging, and soon, all the turtle friends came to thank her for saving their lives.

"You saved us from a big flood," Tilly heard several turtles say to her. "Thank you so much!"

Tilly was once again the happiest turtle in the world, knowing that she had just saved the lives of her friends.

Just for Fun Activity

Tilly the Turtle is thrilled no matter what happens to her. Tell a story of what makes you happy.

Tilly the Turtle is the happiest turtle in the world. The reason she is so comfortable is that she doesn't have a care in the world. She is free to roam the countryside and go wherever she likes.

"I think I want to meet a crocodile," Tilly told her brother Billy the Turtle one day.

"Why do you want to meet a crocodile?" asked Billy.

"Just to be different," said Tilly.

"Well," said Billy. "That would be in the class of something different. Aren't you scared of their large teeth?"

"Oh," said Tilly. "They have large teeth?"

"Yes," said Billy. "They have enormous teeth."

Billy watched as Tilly's smile that she had on her face started to turn upside down.

"You are making me scared," said Tilly.

"Well," said Billy. "Because you are a turtle, you don't have much to worry about."

"Why do you say that?" asked Tilly. "Are you saying that a crocodile wouldn't eat a turtle?"

"Oh," said Billy. "I think they would if they could, but they can't."

Tilly thought about what Billy had just said, and then she suddenly clued into what Billy was getting at. She could easily hide from the crocodile in her shell.

"I guess in that case, I don't need to be scared," said Tilly.

Tilly decided she was going to meet a crocodile. She thought about where she could find one.

"I can't go find one in a supermarket or a mall," said Tilly. "I can't find one out in the streets. Where am I going to find a crocodile?"

"Why don't you go look in the zoo," said Billy. "I bet you would find one there."

"The zoo!" exclaimed Tilly. "Why didn't I think of that?"

Tilly walked to the zoo. She was singing and dancing all the way there.

She was a very happy turtle.

"Hello, Mr. Crocodile," said Tilly when she saw the crocodile exhibit.

The very first thing the crocodile did was show Tilly his big teeth. Tilly immediately hid in her shell.

"Now," said Tilly, looking at the crocodile from her shell. "What did you do that for? That was very mean, showing me your teeth. All I wanted was to be your friend."

"You wanted to be my friend," said the crocodile. "Why would you want to be my friend?"

"I want to be friends with everyone," said Tilly.

"I see," said the crocodile. "I am sorry for showing you my teeth. Do you think you could forgive me?"

"Yes," said Tilly. "I think I can forgive you as long as you don't do that again."

"Okay," said the crocodile. "I promise I won't do that again."

Tilly and the crocodile became the best of friends after that first meeting, and Tilly was pleased.

Tilly the Turtle is the happiest turtle in the world. She is delighted because she has many friends and all of her friends are very special to her.

"I think I want to go make a new friend today," said Tilly to her brother, Billy the Turtle.

"Who do you want to make friends with?" asked Billy.

"I think I want to make friends with a lobster," said Tilly.

"A lobster!" laughed Billy. "That is pretty funny!"

"Why is it funny?" asked Tilly.

“There aren’t too many creatures in this world that want to be friends with a lobster,” explained Billy.

“That is precisely why I want to be friends with a lobster,” said Tilly.

“You do know that they have sharp pinchers on their front claws,” said Billy. “They could snap their pinchers at you and hurt you.”

“I suppose they could try to do that,” said Tilly. “But I could then just hide in my shell.”

“I suppose that is true,” said Billy.

Tilly decided that she wanted to be friends with a lobster.

“Now,” said Tilly. “Where am I going to find a lobster to be friends with? I won’t find one in a library, and I certainly won’t find one in a forest.”

“No,” said Billy. “Tilly, you are silly. Don’t you know that you would have to go to the ocean to find a lobster?”

“Oh yes,” said Tilly, suddenly remembering that the ocean would be the best place to find a lobster.

Tilly left the next morning to find the ocean. Her brother told her to walk in a straight line, either east or west, and she would eventually get to an ocean. He said to her that if she walked to the east, the sea would be closer to her than if she walked to the west.

“I think I will walk east then,” said Tilly.

It was a few days before the smell of the ocean hit Tilly's nostrils. Tilly followed that smell until she came to a sandy beach that ran for miles. She walked to the water's edge, and just by chance, she saw a lobster bobbing up and down in the ocean.

"Oh dear!" exclaimed Tilly, when the first thing the lobster did was stick his pincher in her face.

Tilly immediately hid in her shell. She watched as the lobster couldn't figure out where Tilly had gone to.

"What did you do that for?" asked Tilly, from inside her shell. "You are mean for showing me your pinchers. I came a long way just to be your friend."

"I am sorry," said the lobster. "Nobody has ever wanted to be my friend."

"I want to be everyone's friend," said Tilly. "I accept your apology."

Tilly and the lobster talked for quite some time. The lobster introduced Tilly to a few of his ocean friends, such as an octopus and a sea horse. Tilly was happy to meet them all.

The lobster and Tilly became great friends, and Tilly walked all the way home. She was delighted.

Tilly the Turtle is the happiest turtle in the world. She is happy because nothing in life bothers her. She is carefree and very independent, and she enjoys her life to the fullest. One small thing does worry her, though, and that is when a black bug lands on her nose.

Tilly was out for her usual morning stroll, and she decided she would stop and rest at a big pine tree. Just out of the blue, Tilly jumped ten feet in the air. A black bug had landed right on the end of her nose. It scared her because she wasn't expecting it.

"Why did you land on my nose?" asked Tilly, staring at the black bug with both eyes, almost going cross-eyed in the process.

"It was an accident," said the black bug. "I meant to land on your back. I wanted to hitch a ride with you."

"A ride!" exclaimed Tilly. "That is no way to get a ride."

"I do realize that now," said the black bug.

"Where did you think you were going to get a ride to?" asked Tilly. "I was planning on sleeping for a few hours."

"Oh, nowhere in particular," said the black bug. "I just wanted a ride."

"I see," said Tilly. "Most times, when someone wants a ride, they do have a destination in mind. How come you don't know where you are going?"

"Well," said the black bug. "I did want to visit with the rest of my family, but they are so far away. It would have taken me days to get to them if I flew."

"Where do they live?" asked Tilly. "Across the ocean?"

"No," said the black bug. "They just live on the other side of this forest."

"I see," said Tilly. "I hear there is lots of fresh grass to eat on the other side of the forest, so hop on, and I will take you."

Tilly started walking, and the black bug jumped onto her back. It was a bit slippery, and he was having a bit of a struggle holding on. Tilly walked and walked and, after about an hour of steady walking, it seemed to the black bug that they hadn't gotten very far.

"I could fly faster than this," complained the black bug.

"You probably could," said Tilly. "Why are you so slow?" asked the black bug.

"I am slow because I am a turtle," said Tilly. "All turtles are slow."

The black bug was getting fed up with Tilly's lack of speed. He jumped off her back and flew away.

"Gee," said Tilly. "I guess he wanted to get there in a hurry. He should have said something to me. I would have told him it would have been faster for him to fly."

"Who would you have told?" asked Tilly's brother, Billy.

Tilly told Billy about the black bug.

"Oh, dear!" exclaimed Billy, laughing. "He sure picked the wrong animal to try to hitch a ride with!"

"Yes," said Tilly, also laughing. "He sure did!"

Tilly the Turtle is the happiest turtle in the world. She might not be a speedy turtle, but she is the most comfortable.

"I think I am the slowest turtle in the world," said Tilly, while she was walking along the beach and watching all the other turtles pass her, including her brother, Billy.

"I bet you are the slowest animal in the world," laughed Billy.

"Do you think so?" asked Tilly.

"I am not 100% certain," said Billy. "But it would be pretty close to it."

Billy slowed down his pace and walked alongside Tilly to keep her company. Tilly happened to walk right by a snail.

"Did I just pass that snail?" asked Tilly.

"Yes," said Billy, looking back and seeing the snail behind them.

"Then I guess I am not the slowest animal in the world," said Tilly.

"No," said Billy. "I guess you are not. Why don't you and the snail race? That way, you could be sure you aren't the slowest."

"Okay," said Tilly. "That sounds like fun."

Tilly and Billy talked to the snail, and the snail agreed that they would race.

"On your mark, get set, go!" exclaimed Billy.

The snail took a few steps, and then Tilly took a few steps. It was a pretty slow race with both animals taking it very slowly.

"You won!" exclaimed Billy to his sister when he saw her front claw go over the finish line first.

"I did!" exclaimed Tilly, amazed that there was someone slower than her. "You didn't win by much," said Billy. "However, you did win."

Tilly was so happy, and she enjoyed herself in the race. She enjoyed the thrill and excitement.

"I want to have another race," said Tilly.

"You do know that if you were to race anyone else," said Billy. "You probably would never win."

"I do know that," said Tilly. "It isn't so much the fact that I won. It is the thrill and excitement of just being in the race."

"Okay," said Billy. "Why don't you and I race?"

Tilly and Billy raced while the snail watched. Billy was quite a distance ahead of Tilly initially, but she just kept on with her slow but steady pace.

"Tilly!" exclaimed the snail, watching as Tilly got to the finish line first. "You won! You beat Billy!"

"I can't believe this!" exclaimed Tilly. "I feel so good. I want to race again and again."

Tilly was a very happy turtle.

Zane the Zebra

Zane the Zebra lived in a zoo in a remote little northern town. He was the only zebra the zoo had, and everyone at the zoo loved him. Everyone that is, except for one monkey, Caleb, who was very jealous of him.

"Why is Caleb always so mean to me?" Zane asked his best friend, Harry the Hippo.

"I think he is jealous of you," said Harry.

"Jealous," said Zane. "That is crazy. Why would he be jealous of me?"

“Zane!” exclaimed one of the zookeepers. “I hear that Caleb wants to challenge you to a contest.”

“What kind of contest?” asked Zane.

“A dancing competition,” said the zookeeper.

“What!” exclaimed Zane. “I can’t dance.”

“That is the whole idea,” said the zookeeper. “Caleb knows that he can win this competition because he is a good dancer.”

“Well,” said Zane. “That hardly sounds like a fair competition.”

Zane talked to Harry at great length about the dance competition. At first, Harry thought the same way as Zane, but then he noticed Zane walking away from him toward the barn. It struck him that Zane took up the little walkway with the dainty steps that perhaps Zane could dance.

“Wait up!” exclaimed Harry. “Go tell that zookeeper that you are going to dance in that competition.”

“Are you serious?” asked Zane, thinking that Harry was entirely out of his mind.

“As a matter of fact,” said Harry. “I am serious, and I am going to teach you how to dance.”

“You are?” asked Zane.

“Yes,” said Harry. Harry showed Zane a couple of dance moves. Zane did reasonably well on his first try.

"Good work," said Harry. "You just need to practice."

Zane practiced, and he added a couple of his twists to the dance, which was spectacular.

"Wow!" exclaimed Harry on their second dance lesson. "Zane, you dance exactly like that at the competition, and you are going to win it hands down."

Harry and Zane walked over to the barn where Caleb was waiting with the zookeeper. Caleb was dancing around the barn. He was full of himself with confidence.

"Okay," said the zookeeper. "I think Caleb should go first so we can see what a real dancer looks like."

"Suit yourself," said Zane, looking at Harry and winking.

Caleb did a rather dull dance. It was a step forward, a little twirl, and a step back.

"Okay," said Caleb, once his dance was completed. "It is time to show us your dance."

Harry started the upbeat music, and despite himself, Caleb found himself tapping his tail and left foot to the music. Zane started twirling right away, and he backed up onto his back feet, kicking his front feet in the air. He twisted some more and then did a couple of light steps and kicked up his heels.

At the end of Zane's dance, there was a large eruption of applause as Zane turned around. He didn't realize that all the zoo animals were there watching the competition.

"You did amazing!" exclaimed Harry, very proud of his dance student.

"Caleb," said the zookeeper. "I am afraid to admit this, but Zane's dance was spectacular. He won this competition."

Caleb didn't know what to say, but he knew that the zookeeper was right. He knew that Zane had won the competition. He went over to Zane and shook paws with him. He had no hard feelings, but he did want Zane to teach him a couple of his dance moves.

"Sure," said Zane. "I can do that."

Zane did teach Caleb some of his dance moves, and Caleb was very grateful to Zane. The two became the best of friends.

Zane, the Zebra, was talking to his friend Harry the Hippo. They were discussing the usual things that zoo animals discuss, weather and their food.

"It is scorching out today," said Zane.

"Oh yes, it is," said Harry.

"I guess Humphrey the Camel will like this weather," said Zane, wiping the sweat off his forehead.

"I suppose he would," said Harry. "He is a desert animal."

Humphrey came up behind Zane and Harry, and he was very content in the heat.

“You don’t even have a bead of sweat on your forehead,” said Zane. “How can you stand being outside in this heat?”

“I just can,” said Humphrey. “I am made for this type of weather.”

Zane and Harry were so hot that they had to find a pool of water to cool off.

“Do you want to come to the pool of water with us?” asked Harry. “We need to cool off.”

“I will come with you,” said Humphrey.

Zane, Harry, and Humphrey went to the pool of water. Humphrey was surprised at the number of animals that were just standing in the water, pouring it onto their heads to keep cool.

“Humphrey,” said Zane after a few minutes of being in the nice cool water. “Do you want to come into the water with us? It is nice and cool in here.”

“No, thanks,” said Humphrey. “I am fine.”

All the animals in the pool of water asked Humphrey the same thing. They all got the same answer.

“I am fine,” said Humphrey.

Humphrey enjoyed watching all the other animals in the water. They were laughing and throwing water at themselves.

“That sure looks like fun,” said Humphrey.

“It is a lot of fun,” said Zane. “I know you don’t need to come to the water, but you could come and have some fun with us.”

“Yes,” said Humphrey. “I do suppose I could.”

Humphrey stood in the water, and he did have to admit that the water's coolness did feel good.

“I can see why you all like to stand in the water on a scorching day,” said Humphrey.

Zane splashed some water on Humphrey in a playful manner, and Humphrey sprinkled some on Zane. Soon Humphrey was just as wet as all the other animals.

“Well,” said the zookeeper who came to round up all the animals at the end of the day. “It never ceases to amaze me. I thought camels could stand being in the heat.”

“I love the heat,” said Humphrey.

“You could have fooled me,” said the zookeeper, helping Humphrey out of the water.

“I wasn’t in the water to cool down,” said Humphrey. “When all the other animals were there playing in the water, it just looked like so much fun, and I wanted to have fun with them.”

"I suppose that is true," said the zookeeper. "It does look like fun."

The zookeeper told Humphrey to stay put for a few minutes. Humphrey did as he was told. He watched as the zookeeper went over to the pool of water, and then Humphrey noticed the zookeeper dove right in!

"Wait," said Humphrey. "If you are going into the water, then so am I."

All of the animals had fun splashing the zookeeper with the cool water.

"That was so much fun," said the zookeeper when he finally got out of the water. "I can see why you wanted to play in the water, Humphrey."

On the very hottest days at the zoo, many of the animals and the zookeeper would be at the water pool splashing water around at each other. They all had a lot of fun together.

Zane the Zebra was sitting under a tall tree because it was nice and cool there in the shade. It was a sweltering day at the zoo.

"I am sweltering today," said Zane to his friend, Harry the Hippo.

"It is scorching hot today," said Harry. "I wonder if Allie the Alligator is too hot to play any of her tricks on us."

"I sure hope so," said Zane. "She always tries to sneak up on us while we are in the water."

"Allie knows we have to go into the water in this heat so that we can cool down too," said Harry.

"That is exactly why she tries to trick us," said Zane. "What if we decided we weren't going to go into the water? Then she would have nobody to sneak upon. Would she?"

"That is a good idea," said Harry. "What if all the animals stayed away from the water for one full day?"

"I bet Allie would miss us," said Zane.

"Yes," said Harry. "I think that is true, and then if she misses us," said Harry. "Then maybe she would stop trying to trick us."

Zane and Harry went around to all the animals and told them to stay away from the water that next day. They all agreed.

"Where is everyone?" asked Allie when she realized she was the only one in the water. "It is a scorching day, and this water should be packed with animals."

Allie swam around the water, and she noticed that it was just too quiet, and she didn't like the quietness. She also felt very lonely, and she didn't like that feeling either.

"Why isn't anyone here with me?" asked Allie. "I miss everyone."

Allie thought and thought very hard about why there were no other animals in the water with her.

"Maybe it was me," thought Allie to herself. "Maybe I was too mean to everyone."

Allie thought back to the day before and how when Zane came to the water, she had gone right up to him and stuck her nose right on his, scaring him. She thought of how Zane and Harry were talking while standing in the water, and she thought of how she swam right between the two and splashed her tail at the two of them.

"I guess maybe it is me that they are avoiding," said Allie. "What have I done?"

Allie walked out of the water, and she found Zane and Harry by the barn.

"I am sorry for scaring you two yesterday," said Allie.

"Do you miss us?" asked Zane.

"Yes," said Allie truthfully. "I do miss you very much."

"Do you promise not to scare us anymore?" asked Harry. "Yes," said Allie.

"I do promise. I don't like being in the water all by myself. It is too lonely."

Zane and Harry told all the other animals that they could go back into the water. Allie was charming to all of them, and they all got along very well.

Zane the Zebra was outside of the barn, and he heard a strange noise.

"What is that noise?" asked Zane. "It is scaring me."

"What noise?" said Zane's best friend, Harry the Hippo.

"I heard something," said Zane. "It sounded like someone or something was saying something, but there is nobody here. I looked all around, and I couldn't see anyone or anything."

"Maybe it was an owl," said Harry. "They like to make noises."

"Maybe," said Zane.

Zane continued to hear different sounds all that day, and he just couldn't figure out where they were coming from. He was standing beside the bird exhibit, so he thought maybe it was an owl, although he couldn't see an owl, and as far as he knew, there was no owl at the zoo.

Zane walked through the bird exhibit, and he could still hear the noises.

"You still look scared," said Harry. "I take it the noises haven't stopped yet."

"No," said Zane, quite annoyed by the noises. "They haven't stopped."

"We need to find out what is making the noises," said Harry.

"How can we find that out?" asked Zane.

"What we can do is try to eliminate what is not making the noise," said Harry. "That way, we can try to narrow it down to what is making the noise."

"That is a good idea," said Zane. "How do we do that?"

"Okay," said Harry. "Let's take a good look around us. Do you hear the noise right now?"

"Yes," said Zane. "I do."

"Okay," said Harry. "So, do you see an owl anywhere around you right now?"

"No," said Zane, taking a good look. "I do not see an owl."

"Okay," said Harry. "Now tell me what you do see."

"Well," said Zane. "I see a monkey walking around his cage."

"Okay," said Harry. "Do you think the monkey would make the noise you hear?"

"No," said Zane.

"Okay," said Harry. "What else do you see?"

"I see a crow," said Zane.

“Do you think a crow would make that noise you are hearing?” asked Harry.

Zane took a close look at the crow. He saw the crow sitting very still and then all of a sudden he did know the crow move its beak and he heard noises, the very same noises he had been hearing.

“It is the crow making those noises,” said Zane.

“That is good that we figured that one out,” said Harry. “Now, are you still scared?”

“No,” said Zane. “I’m not.”

Zane was never frightened of noises after that day. He would always take a close look around him and try to figure out what was causing the noise first before getting scared about them.

Zane, the Zebra, was walking through the zoo's grounds, and he noticed something standing in the field just ahead.

“That looks like an elephant,” said Zane.

Harry the Hippo, Zane’s best friend, also noticed the elephant.

“We have an elephant at the zoo now,” said Zane.

“It appears that way,” said Harry. “I like elephants,” said Zane.

“So do I,” said Harry.

Zane and Harry introduced themselves to the elephant.

“I am Lydia,” said the elephant.

"It is nice to meet you," said Zane and Harry at the same time.

"It is nice to meet you too," said Lydia. "I am looking forward to being the mascot for the zoo."

"A mascot?" asked Zane, to Harry, later that day. "What did Lydia mean by that?"

"A mascot is a symbol that brings good luck to the zoo," said Harry.

"Oh," said Zane. "How come they didn't choose me to be the mascot?"

"Well," said Harry, who knew this question was coming. "Have you brought good luck to the zoo?"

Zane thought long and hard about that question, and he knew that he had to admit that he hadn't.

"No," said Zane, honestly. "I haven't."

Zane and Harry walked around the zoo, and they were watching everyone as they all flocked over to see Lydia. People were so excited to see her.

"Look at all the attention that Lydia is getting," said Zane.

"I think you are jealous of Lydia," said Harry.

"No," said Zane quickly.

Zane thought about what Harry had just said. Maybe he was jealous of Lydia. After all, he could have made an excellent mascot for the zoo.

“Maybe I am jealous,” admitted Zane, holding his head down.

“There is nothing to be jealous about,” said Harry. “Lydia didn’t do anything.”

“Yes,” said Zane. “That is very true.”

Zane decided he would support Lydia being the mascot. He did feel so much better about it.

“I don’t know why I am being chosen for the mascot,” said Lydia one day.

“You do make a good mascot,” said Zane.

“You know,” said Lydia. “You have been very supportive of me, and I appreciate it.”

“I have to admit that I was jealous of you to start with,” said Zane.

“I am glad you aren’t now,” said Lydia. “Are you coming to the ceremony tomorrow?”

“Yes,” said Zane. “I will be there.”

Zane and Harry were at the ceremony, and it was time for Lydia to make a speech.

"I appreciate being chosen as your mascot," said Lydia. "However, I think you have a much more deserving mascot in your midst. I think that Zane should be your mascot."

The zoo officials thought about Lydia's suggestion, and the more they thought about it, the more they liked the idea.

"Okay," said Mr. Brown, the head zoo official. "We do have to agree with Lydia. We are therefore going to make Zane our official zoo mascot!"

Zane was beside himself. He was delighted, and because of the jealousy he felt to- ward, Lydia initially decided that he would not let his pride stand in his way and that he would be the best mascot he could be.

Just for Fun Activity

Zane the Zebra has distinctive stripes that make him stand out from other animals. What is the one feature about yourself that makes you stand out from other people? Being different in your way is a good thing!

William's Adventures

Going for Fishing

One summer, William's father was home for five weeks. On one particular Friday, he said to William, "How about you and me going fishing up to Big Lake." William looked at his father and said, "Really, daddy?" "Sure. We will get up early and spend the weekend up there. Okay?"

William jumped up and down and ran to his room. “Where are you going?” his father asked. “I have to get ready.” Said, William. William looked in his toy box in his room and pulled out a flashlight, king toy, and a hat. When his father came in, he said, “You better get a jacket too. It can get cool there at night.” William’s father went i9nto the garage, and William followed him. His father opened a cabinet and grabbed the tent that was folded there.

Then he picked out two fishing poles and a tackle box that held the hooks and bobbers. “I think that all we need now is our backpacks and some food to put in them.” Said William’s father. When his mother came home, William ran to her and said, “We're going fishing, mommy.” “We are not. You and daddy are. I am staying home and cleaning up the mess you made in your room.” She said, smiling at him. William said, “Gosh, mommy. I’m sorry. I’ll help clean it tonight a little.”

And so he did. Although he only put his toys away in the toy box. William couldn’t fall asleep because he thought about the fishing trip in the morning. Slowly his eyes closed, and then he dreamed about catching fish. The next morning his father came into his room very early. William was still sleeping, and his father woke him and said, “Come on, William. We have to go.” So William got out of bed and dressed in a hurry. He dressed so fast he put his shoes on the wrong feet and buttoned his shirt wrong. “Hold on,

William. Let me help." Told his father when he saw Williams's shirt.

When they were ready, William and his father went out to the car. His father had packed everything the night before and said goodbye to William's mother and drove off. They stopped at a small restaurant along the way, and William ate some pancakes, and his father had coffee and a donut. When they got to Big Lake, William helped his father set up the tent and put their things inside. The lake was right there, so they took their fishing poles and

I started fishing. William watched his father as he put a worm on the hook. William said, "Can I try daddy?" but his father said, "You can give me a worm, and I will put it on the hook for you, William. Okay?" "Okay, daddy." And William reached into the bag of worms and grabbed one wiggling in his hands.

"Ugh, this thing is slippery." Said, William. And he gave it to his father. The day wore on, and the fish didn't want to bite on the hooks. William was getting tired of just sitting there. He said to his father, "Daddy, when will I catch a fish?" his father laughed and said, "Well, William, you have to ask the fish that. I don't know." All of s sudden, Williams, there was a tug on Williams's pole. "Daddy!" said William. "It's alright, William. Just let him grab some more." "How do you know it's him, daddy?" said William. "That's just what you sometimes say, William."

There was another tug on the pole, only a little harder this time. Then the rod bent down, and William's father said, "That's it, William. Now pull him in." and William raised his fishing pole, and out of the water came a fish stuck on his rod. "Wow. I got a fish, daddy." Said, William. The fish jumped up and down and tried to get away, but William's father caught hold of Williams's fish line and took the fish off. He showed it to William and then said, "Now we let him go again, William."

William looked at his father and said, "Why?" his father said, "If we keep him and don't beat him, that is cruel to the fish. We let him go so that he will live for someone else to catch him again later." William said he understood, and his father put the fish back into the lake. Their day went on, and they caught a few more fish until the sun was low in the sky. That night William and his father slept in the tent, and William dreamed of the fish and how he was so happy to be let go again.

The next day after breakfast, they cleaned up the campgrounds and put the tent away. When they came home, it was getting dark, and William went into his mother and said, "Mommy, I caught a fish, and then we let him go again because he wanted to be with his friends." His mother hugged him and then said, "You need a bath, mister. You smell like fish." And so William's first fishing trip was a success. He was happy, and so were his mother and father.

Going to the Doctor

Before William could go to kindergarten, he had to be cleared by a doctor. His mother tried to prepare him for a visit by telling him everything that the doctor would do. William knew that the doctor would not hurt him but was there to help keep him healthy. “I am not afraid of the doctor.” He said proudly to his king doll.

Of course, the doll didn’t answer, but William knew he understood. William pretended to be the doctor and examined his beauty. He looked at his feet than the hands and head saying, “Open your mouth.” But the doll again just looked at him. When the day arrived, William was all excited. In the car on the way there, he was asking his mother all kinds of questions. “How far is it to the doctor, mommy?”

"When will we get there?" "Is the office big?" and his mother answered all of them with a smile. When they came to the building, William no longer was talking. He was a little scared, but he took his mother's hand and walked into the office. When they went to the front desk, William looked over the counter at the women there. She was dressed in a white dress and had a little hat on her head. William had never seen anyone dressed like that before, except in the meat market in the store.

The butcher had a white coat on when his mother took him to shop for food. "Are we buying food?" asked William. His mother smiled and said, "No, William, we're here to see the doctor so that you can go to school. Remember?" "Oh!" said William. "Are you the doctor?" asked William to the nurse. "No. I'm a nurse. I help the doctor." She answered. William and his mother sat down on a couch, and his mother read a magazine. William looked at the other people in the room, waiting for the doctor.

"Are all these people going to school, too?" asked William. His mother laughed and said, "No, William. I don't think so." William sat close to his mother. After a while, William said, "When are we going to see the doctor?" his mother said, "When it's our turn." So William sat back and played with the king toy that he brought with him. He said to it, "We have to wait for our turn." And put him down next to him on the couch. When almost everyone else was gone, the door opened, and the nurse came out. "William?" she said. William looked at her, and his mother got up and took

William's hand was leading him into the other room. William looked around at all the machines there. His mother picked him up and put him on something that looked like a bed but had no blanket. William dangled his legs over the side, swinging them back and forth. The nurse put something around his arm and pumped it up until William felt the pressure.

She looked like earphones to William in her ear and touched William's arm with something cold. Then she put a stick into his mouth made of glass. William had to stay real still until she took it out again. When she was done, she said as she left the room, "The doctor will be right in." William couldn't stay still for very long. The door opened again, and the doctor came in. "Are you the doctor?" asked William.

"Why, yes, I am William. How do you feel today?" William looked at the doctor and said, "Fine." "That's good. The nurse said that everything looks good. Let me listen to your heart. Okay, William?" and the doctor put on those ear things and touched his tummy with it." That sounds very good too." Said the doctor.

The doctor told William to open his mouth, and the doctor looked in. Then he helped William down and told him to walk to the door and back, and William did what the doctor said. When he was done, he talked to William's mother.

"Everything looks great." And he gave Williams mother a slip of paper. When they left the office, William said to his mother, "Can I go to school now, mommy?" his mother said to William, "Yes dear, you can go to school now but not today." William was glad that the doctor took such good care of him.

Halloween

One of the best holidays that William loved was Halloween. William's mother dressed him up in a different costume every year. Last year she dressed him as a hobo with black cheeks and an old coat that was too big for him.

He wore his father's shoes, also too big and torn pants. He looked into a mirror, and they all laughed at what they saw. About a week before the big day, William knew it was near and went to his mother and said, "What can I be this year for Halloween?" his mother stopped what she was doing and sat down with William at her side.

"What would you like to be?" she asked him. "I don't know, mommy." "Well, what do you like to play a lot?" she asked again. William thought hard, and then his eyes got big. "I know. I want to be a cowboy."

His mother shook her head and smiled. "Okay." She said to him. When the day came, William could hardly wait any longer. "Mommy, can I dress up now so we can go trick or treating?" William's mother said, "All right, William. Let me get your clothes." And she went to the closet and picked out the cowboy outfit that she made for him.

There were a cowboy hat and pants with a shirt that looked like the real cowboys' clothes on TV. "Oh, boy." Said William as he started to put them on. His mother helped, and soon, he was all dressed up. When he was done, he ran to his father, who was reading the paper, and said, “Daddy, will you take me trick or treating?” his father put the form down and looked at William.

“William, you can’t go out like that.” He said. William didn’t know what to say. He looked down and said, “Why not, daddy?” his father stood up and walked to the hall closet. William just watched him.

When his father came back, he had a box in his hands. He gave the box to William, who opened it. Inside were the best cowboy boots that William had ever seen. “Wow!” was all that William could say.

“Now, with those on, we are ready to go trick or treating.” Said his father. William put the boots on, and the three of them walked out the front door. William had a shopping bag that had a picture of a pumpkin on it.

“I am going to fill this up with all the candy I can get.” He proclaimed. After about an hour, they came home again. William had received a lot of candy, and his mother was looking at it to make sure that it would be okay for

William. All William wanted to do was eat the candy and couldn’t wait. He kept jumping around the table as his mother sorted out the candy. Finally, she gave some to William. “Now you have to save some for the rest of the week, William.” His mother said. “Okay, mommy. But you can have some too.”

His father heard this and said, “What about me, champ?” William laughed and said, “Sure, daddy. But leave some for me too.”

Washing the Car

It is always fun for William to help his father do things around the house. One Sunday, after church, William's father went into William's room. "William. Would you like to help me wash the car?" he said. William dropped his toys and went to his closet. He still had on his right clothes for church.

"I have to put on my car washing clothes, daddy." Said, William. He looked at all his clothes until his father came over and picked out some pants and a shirt for him. William hurried to put on the clothes and then ran out the front door. His father said, “William, get the bucket in the garage, please.”

As he pulled the hose out to the car. William came back with the bucket and gave it to his father, saying, “Here, daddy.” When William’s father put soap into the bucket, he said to William, “Go and turn on the water William.” And William went over to the faucet and turned the hose on.

The water sputtered as the air in the hose was pushed out by the water. William laughed when he saw the hose jump with the air and water coming out. His father filled the bucket up, and soon, and they had soapy water for the car. William put the sponge into the bucket then, taking it out, started to rub the sponge onto the vehicle.

His father also took a sponge and did the top of the car. When William had put enough soap on the car, his father used the hose to wash the soap off. “Here, William. You do this a while.” And he gave the hose to him.

William ran the water over the car where he had put the soap on and then tried to wash off the soap where his father had put it. “Whoa there, cowboy.” Said his father. William’s father liked to call him a cowboy. William lowered the hose, and his father took it and finished the top of the car.

“What do we do now?” asked William. His father went into the garage, brought out two pieces of leather, and gave one to

William. “Now we dry the car.” He said. “Okay, daddy.” Said William, and he started to rub the water off the car. Soon the car was dry, and William said, “Boy daddy.

The car is all sparkly.” “Yes, William. You did a fantastic job.” William ran into the house and went to his mother. “Mommy. We washed the car, and I helped daddy, and it looks shiny. Come outside and see.” Said, William. So his mother took William’s hand, and they went

outside. “Your right William. It looks beautiful.” Said his mother. When everything was put away, William’s father said, “Let’s take a ride in the car now that it’s all cleaned up.” So they got into the car and drove to town.

William’s father stopped at the candy store and bought William an ice cream cone. “Here, William. That’s for helping me wash the car.” William was pleased. “When can we rewash it, daddy?” said William. “Why don’t we let it get dirty first, William.” Said his father with a laugh. Then they all laughed as they drove back home.

Going to a Drive-In Movie

One day William's father came home and said to William's mother, "How about a movie tonight?" then his mother said, "I don't think I can get a babysitter." "We can go to the drive-in, and William can go too." Said his father.

When William heard that he was going to a movie, he jumped up and down until his mother finally said, "Okay. I guess we can. William has been excellent today so that he can go with us." That's all William needed. He went into his closet and got a jacket to wear. When he came into the kitchen wearing the coat, his mother said, "We're not going until it gets dark, William. We will eat dinner first, and then we can go."

So William took off the jacket but left it over his chair to put it on as soon as everyone was ready. When it started to get dark out, William went to his father and asked, "Now can we go, daddy?" and his father said, "Yes, I think it's time, William." William went to his mother and said, "Daddy said it's time to go, mommy." His mother got her jacket, and William put on his coat and walked out to the car. William was all excited and kept asking if they were there yet, and his father said, "Almost William."

When they got to the drive-in, there was a line of cars waiting to get in. William's father moved up slowly until it was their turn to pay. "Two, please." Said William's father. William said, "What about me?" his father said, "You don't have to pay yet, William. Maybe next year. They drove on ways until William's father turned the car to face the large screen. Then he took a speaker and pulled it onto the window of the vehicle. William could hardly wait, but soon, the movie started.

First, there were some cartoons that William liked. After the comics, the movie started. William watched for a while, but soon it began to get boring, and he played with his king toy. “Do you like this movie?” he asked the toy, which only stared back at him through his painted eyes.

After a while, William grew tired, and soon, he was asleep in the car's back seat. He didn’t even wake up until his mother was putting him in his bed back at home. “Was the movie good?” he said to his mother. He could hardly keep his eyes open. “Yes, dear. It was perfect.” She said as she kissed him goodnight. She turned off the light as William took his king toy and turned over back to sleep.

Making Cookies

William was playing in the yard one day when his mother called to him. "William. Come in. I have something for you." She said. William came into the kitchen and asked, "What do you have for me, mommy?" William's mother showed him a cookbook. There on the open page were cookies.

"Wow, mommy. Can I have some of those cookies?" asked William. "First, we have to bake them." She said. "Can I help?" asked William again. His mother put her hands on her hips and said, "I guess so." She went to the pantry and took out an apron to wear.

"Here," She said to William as she held out another apron to him. William put it on. It was a little too big for him, but his mother tied it up to fit William better. "First, we have to measure out the flour. Then we can add the other things to make the cookies." She said to William. William held the flour bag and poured some out into a measuring cup. Some spilled on the table, but his mother said, "It's all right, William. We can clean up when we're finished."

After mixing the ingredients, she took a spoon and, scooping up some of the batters, placed some on a cookie sheet. Then she gave William the knife and said, "Would you like to lick the spoon?" William took the spoon and tasted the batter. It was good, so he put the whole knife into his mouth. "Yummy!" he said. His mother smiled and then put the cookie sheet into the oven.

William sat on a chair in front of the oven, looking at the baking cookies. When the timer bell rang, William went and got his mother in the laundry room. "The bell rang, mommy." He told her.

His mother went into the kitchen, took the cookies out of the oven, and put them on the counter to cool. "When can I have a cookie, mommy?" he asked. His mother said, "When they are cool enough. Maybe in two or three minutes." So William waited in the chair next to the cookies, all the while asking his mother again and again, "Now."

When the cookies were cool enough, William's mother gave him some cookies. "These are great." Said William between bites. By the time he finished the last cookie, William was full. "I can't eat anymore." He said to his mother. He took his king doll and went outside to play.

Going to the Library

One afternoon William's mother asked him if he would like to go to the library because there would be a reading of a book for children that day. "What will they read?" asked William. "I don't know, but I bet it will be interesting." She said. After they had some lunch, William and his mother drove to the library.

William took his mother's hand, and they walked into the library. William had never been in the library and looked around at everything. He had brought along his king doll and held it up and said, "Mommy said we have to be real quiet in the library, so don't say anything."

The doll looked at him as usual, and William's mother laughed at what William said to his beauty. They walked up to the check-out counter, and William's mother said, "Where should we go to hear the children's story time?"

The woman behind the counter said, “That will be downstairs in the children’s section.”

So William and his mother went downstairs to the children’s section. As they walked over to the area where some children and mothers were already seated, William let his mother’s hand go and ran over to a boy he knew. “Hi.” Said, William. The boy stood up and said hi to William, and the two sat down in front of the other children.

After a while, a young woman came from behind the children’s section. He sat on the chair in front of William. She held up a book and said, “Today I am going to read a story about pirates and buried gold. Can anyone tell me how a pirate looks?” asked the young woman. William put his hand up. “Yes.” said the women pointing to William. “He has a cover over his eye and wears a funny hat.” Said, William.

“That’s right.” She said. “What sound does he make when he is mad?” Again William raised his hand, but this time, someone else said, “Arrrrr.” “You are right again.” William liked this game and sat down as the young woman started to read the pirate story. All the children were quiet as she read.

When the end of the book came, she asked some questions to see if they remembered the story. Everyone did, and then it was time to go. William took his mother’s hand as they walked out to the car. “Mommy, can we come again to the library?” he asked her. “If you behave and keep your room clean, we will come again.”

She said. He could hardly wait to go to the library again. That night when William went to bed, he dreamed about pirates and ships. This would be one of William's favorite games to play in his back yard. He was always the captain and his king toy Gus was his helper.

The Butterfly Search and the Fairy

Episode 1

Chapter 1

It was a great day to go looking for butterflies! The sun was up. The air was crisp. The new net Danny Bundy's dad had given him was empty now. Still, Danny was so excited about the butterflies he was going to find for show-and-tell next Monday.

I could try and bring a bullfrog, Danny thought. *But every boy gets a bullfrog or a scared squirrel in a cage. A bullfrog would be too easy.*

Danny wanted to win the show-and-tell contest this year. He would bring the most giant, most beautiful butterfly in the world and win an awesome pizza party!

Danny slurped down a bowl of cereal.

He filled his backpack with a peanut butter sandwich, chips, and a thermos of milk.

He tipped his cap and said goodbye to his mother.

"Don't go too far, Bundy!" his mother called. "And be back before dark!" His whole life, for whatever reason, his parents had always called him Bundy. Danny smiled at his mother.

"Don't worry, Ma," he said. "I'll be back before you can say, 'Catch that butterfly!'" In a flash, Danny jumped off the back-porch steps, over the wire fence, and into the forest searching for the beautiful monarch butterfly.

Danny was eight years old and short for his age. His classmates teased him about his height, red hair, and freckles, but he didn't pay attention. Danny was smart. He knew he would grow up taller than all of them one day, and his freckles would fade. All he had to do was look at his dad, Walter Bundy.

Danny's dad was the town librarian, the tallest and most handsome man Danny knew. His hair was as red as Danny's, but he had no freckles. And every night since before Danny could remember, Danny's dad had brought home books to share. Danny's dad would read to Danny in the evenings about exciting people and places worldwide. Most of all, Danny enjoyed the books with beautiful pictures of the homes his dad read about. Danny dreamed of visiting those places one day.

Danny's favorite book, though, was a big book about butterflies. The colors and patterns of the butterflies' wings were unique! More than anything, he wanted to see them up close, especially the *Danaus plexippus*: the monarch butterfly. T he first time he saw a picture of a monarch butterfly, he had not been able to look away. He had cried much when his dad closed the book that his dad had put the book under

Danny's pillow for the night. The next day, Danny had been so happy when his dad told him he would order another copy of the book for the library—the document under his pillow was his! Walter Bundy had smiled wide and said to his wife, "Who knows, Maggie? Bundy here may just be the world's youngest lepidopterist." Danny had been three years old.

The forest behind Danny Bundy's house was a great place to ex- plore! The trees seemed to go on forever, and the creeks and gullies held so many secrets! Danny loved playing in the forest. This morning, he had high hopes of finding the butterfly of his dreams. His father had said he would not find a monarch butterfly this early in the year, but Danny did not look- ing for just *any* butterfly.

And, in his mind, he knew anything was possible in the magical forest behind his house. His parents and other kids at school told strange stories about the things that had happened there!

As Danny entered the woods, he noticed the rich, wet smell of the forest floor. Grass, fallen leaves, and other things were decomposing, but the forest smelled like li fe.

Danny stood still a moment, taking in the beauty of the forest. "The butterflies probably need to drink," Danny said to himself. "I'll start looking at the water." He took a deep breath, then started down a hill into a shadowy gully. It led to a bubblin g brook lined with many slippery rocks and pebbles covered with algae.

Danny paused by the brook. Last year, he had tripped on the rocks, and his mother had had to patch up his cuts and two scraped knees. "You're not going to get me this time, brook," Danny said. "I'm going to hop over you like a grasshopper!" Danny jumped and landed safely on the other side. "Where are you, butterflies?" he whispered. "I know you're around here somewhere."

Just then, Danny heard a loud croak from under a large leaf at the edge of the brook. “I know what’s under there,” Danny said. “Just another lousy ol’ bullfrog!” Danny bent down and lifted the leaf. Sure enough, there it was: a giant, fat green-and-gray bullfrog just like the ones all the other boys would bring in for show-and-tell. It seemed to be smiling up at him.

Danny made a face at it. “That’s what I thought,” he said, dis- gusted. “A rotten, dirty old bullfrog that nobody wants to see.” He threw the wet, rotting leaf in his hand back over the frog. He wiped his slimy hands on his shorts. He turned to continue his search for the butterfly.

“Hold on there, young man!” someone shouted. “What did you just say?!”

Danny gasped! He spun around! His heart was jumping as it would hop right out of his chest! But there was no one behind him. With wide, frightened eyes, Danny searched for the person who had shouted at him.

A few seconds passed, and Danny began to calm down. He turned his attention back to the bank of the brook—and the voice spoke again, from under the dead wet leaf! “Right here, sonny!

Yes, me! Did you say I was rotten and dirty? I’ll have you know I take good care of myself! I eat only the best bugs! I drink the cleanest water I can find! And since I live in the water, I’m always clean! So what gives with the bad vibes?” Danny thought someone was playing a trick on him! Had someone followed him down to the brook? But when he looked around, there was no one else—just the leaf, moving with the breaths of the bullfrog beneath. "Take this leaf off me!" the frog ordered.

"I want to see if you're just another rotten, dirty little boy!" Danny wanted to run, but he couldn't leave without his butterfly. So he took a breath and, feeling crazy, spoke to the frog.

"Listen, frog, and I don't believe you can talk. I must be hearing things. My dad says the only animals that can talk are parrots." "'Polly wants a cracker,'" the frog joked. "Listen, kid, and there are things your dad don't know. Hurry up and get this leaf off me, or I'll hop away and leave you to find that butterfly by yourself."

"Butterfly?" Danny repeated, amazed.

"I heard you earlier," the frog explained. "Look, you know this is a *magical* forest, right?"

Danny blinked. "My parents and friends told me stories, but I didn't believe them. I thought it was like the Easter Bunny or the tooth fairy." He couldn't believe this frog could talk!

"Whoa!" the bullfrog cried. "Maybe the Easter Bunny's a story, but watch your mouth about the fairies, hey?" He croaked once. "Could you just take the leaf off? It doesn't smell that good." Danny stared, then slowly bent down and lifted the leaf off the frog.

"Whew!" The frog's throat swelled and shrank. It stared up at Danny with wet, black eyes, blinked, and then hopped right up to his swamp-stained feet. "Thanks," it said. "You know, I don't talk to just anyone. The last time I tried it, this guy tried to catch me with a rag dripping with alcohol!" "How did you get away?" Danny asked. The frog seemed to smile. "I have a few friends that give me a hand from time to time," he boasted, then looked around nervously.

"Hey, have you seen any owls or hawks flying around here? They say we frogs are pretty tasty to them, and I don't want any of them to find out with me." Danny, less afraid now and more impressed by the brave old magical bullfrog, puffed out his chest. "I'll make sure they don't get you!" he promised. "Good, kid. Good.

You know, I still see that guy out here with his rag and his glass jar?" the frog remarked. "But I keep my mouth shut! Yes, sir. Nothing but ribbits out of this old boy! You can bet your life on that!" Danny knelt to get a better look at the strange talking frog. "Why are you talking to me?" The frog blinked. "Well, you just made me so angry," he explained. "But I've seen you down here before with your dad. You were both careful to leave everything, just like you found it.

Didn't even pick up a rock to chuck across the water like the other kids. You don't know how many of my friends have been hurt by that.

"Lot of 'em have turned up missing, too," the frog added thoughtfully. "Every time some little boy wants to show them off in school. Tell me, kid, why is it that when they take us from our homes, they don't think to bring us back? I don't know if we'd mind being taken out for a little while. We're curious, just like everyone else.

Leastways, we could see what's out there, learn something—but every time one of my friends gets picked up, it's a one-way street. He never comes back!" The frog looked suspiciously at Danny. "Tell me, kid, does it have something to do with the alcohol or the jars? Or is it worse?"

Chapter 2:

Danny thought of older kids talking about dissecting dead frogs in science class. It was terrible to think the frogs they cut apart could have been like this one! "Worse," he whispered. He felt sick as the bullfrog stared at him. "I don't know what to say, Mr. Frog."

Seeing how upset Danny was, the bullfrog jumped on his foot in a friendly way.

"Let's not start that. You and *I* can be buds, hey? You can call me Bernardo—or, better yet, Bernie. Yeah, that's good. What should I call you?"

"My name's Danny Bundy. Everyone calls me Bundy." The frog seemed to sniff. "I'll call you, Danny then. I don't want to follow all the rest. Besides, you look like a Danny." Danny was confused. "What does a Danny look like, Bernie?" "Like you, kid, like you," Bernie said, which did not help at all.

Danny went down to the brook and looked at his rippling re- flection. The forest breeze had messed up his hair, and even though the rapids, he could see all of his freckles. "The other kids tease me," he said. "I'm short, and I have a lot of freckles." "Get a good look at me, kid," Bernie said. "I ain't so blemish-free, either. I got bumps as well. But some of the lady frogs around here think I'm a pretty good catch!"

Danny laughed, looking back at Bernie. *He's*
not so ugly, Danny thought. *He's pretty good looking when he s*

miles. "Bernie, can you help me find my butterfly?" Danny asked. Bernie sniffed again.

"What do you mean by *your* butterfly, Danny boy? You should think carefully about what belongs to you before running around in *this* forest.

I think any butterfly you meet might have other plans than being *yours*. But sure, I can introduce you to a few." He looked around thoughtfully. "It's still a little chilly out here. Most of them will always be caterpillars for another month or so, but a few of them might be interested in getting a head start on the nectar.

Let's see what we can find." "Great!" Danny cried. "Tell me where to go, and I'll be on my way!" Bernie paused for a moment. "Maybe I can go with you, kid— I mean, Danny, if you're careful with me. I'm pretty intense down here, but I'm a little nervous about heights.

I don't want to go *splat* if you know what I mean. But we'll move faster and find more together. Could you pick me up? If you don't jiggle or anything while I'm up there, I can ride on your shoulder. Have a better look around to see where we have to go." He looked at Danny. "You won't shake or something if I pick a bug out of the air every so often, will you? I need to eat all the time. I can't let a tender morsel fly on by." Danny smiled. He was happy the frog was coming with him.

"I can share my peanut butter sandwich with you," he offered. Bernie made a face. "Peanut butter?! Yuck! Man, that even sounds wrong!" "Never mind," Danny said, reaching down to pick up Bernie. As gently as he could, he placed the frog on his right shoulder, and the two started on their search.

Danny and Bernie's journey began with a walk down the brook toward a bank of tall trees. They seemed to melt into the fluffy cotton-candy clouds way up high. Bernie was having a blast seeing the world from Danny's shoulder.

He kept telling Danny to turn around so he could see his home from different angles. "Turn that way, Danny. I want to see over that ridge. Would you look at that? Even up here, those trees are still enormous. And the air smells so much better I can't believe it. Turn this way! Turn that way! Hey, standstill.

I want to take it all in." Danny did his best to show his friend the forest as he saw it. He picked up flower petals, leaves, and other things for Bernie to see, taste, and smell. But when they entered the dark thicket ahead, the air became chilly. Danny shivered. Bernie croaked a laugh. "Look at you and your goose bumps!" he teased. "It's like the bumps I have all the time, but you're cold.

What does it feel like, kid?" "It's like snow in my body," Danny said after a moment of thought. "White, ice-cold snow. But it's like the winter holiday— it doesn't feel bad. I'm just happy to be alive, even if the forest is a bit creepy."

Bernie was a bit confused. "Maybe you can tell me about this 'winter holiday' thing," he suggested. Danny did his best to explain how it felt in the winter when school let out. He talked about how families came together and counted their blessings. It made Danny and Bernie feel better as they walked deeper into a part of the forest neither of them had ever seen before. "So you all celebrate this time of year?"

Bernie wanted to know. "In different ways," Danny told the frog. "And there are other celebrations during other times of the year." "It's wonderful you and your family have time to feast and be grateful," Bernie told Danny. "We kinda do the same thing after a good rainy season. We have lots of mosquitoes, flies, and other great things flying around to eat. And we eat and eat and eat and croak out loud cause we're so happy." Bernie pointed with his nose off to Danny's right.

"Hey, let's stop over there by that rotting stump. I'm going reach out to an old friend of mine who's supposed to live around here." Danny lifted Bernie off of his shoulder and set him down on the stump. "Give me a minute, will you, Danny?" Bernie asked. "I gotta take care of some business if you know what I mean. Been holding it in for the longest time."

Danny left Bernie on the stump. He walked around, looking up into the tall trees for monarch butterflies. He was walking be- tween two larger, older trees when a shrill voice barked down at him, "What are you doing here? You! You! You got to go! You got to go!"

There, high, high in the tree, Danny spotted a pair of beady black eyes and a small, whiskered nose poking out at him from a burrow in the side of the trunk. It was a female squirrel. "Don't make me come out there because I will!" she chattered. "I will come out there and make you get gone!" She was terrified,

Danny realized, but she was so brave he smiled. "I don't want to hurt you," he told her. "You don't, do you? I've seen boys like you, with your awful traps and things, taking away all my friends! You take them away, and they never come back!" "I'm not here to take you anywhere!"

Danny protested, spreading his hands wide. "I'm just looking for butterflies." The squirrel did not believe him. She laughed. "You silly! It's too soon for butterflies. Much too soon. Only caterpillars now. Only caterpillars are eating up all the leaves. You won't find any butterflies now, so go away!"

She's much less friendly than Bernie, Danny thought. He took a step back. "OK, OK. I'll leave you alone. I'll just go back to pick up Bernie the bullfrog, and we'll be gone."

"Bullfrog?" The squirrel's tone changed completely, and she ran out of her burrow to stand, quivering, on a branch high above Danny's head. "What do you mean, 'bullfrog'? Where is this bullfrog?"

Danny pointed. "I left him right over there on that stump. If you come with me, I'll introduce you." The squirrel seemed to think. "I met a bullfrog when I was just a kid," she told Danny. "My folks were gone, so he named me Lady Sue." Her tail curled up and over her back. "Not at first. Not at first. At first, he called me 'kid.'"

"That's what Bernie calls me!" Danny cried. "Maybe he's the one you knew before!" The squirrel was curious now. "Yes, I think I will go with you. I want to know if this bullfrog is my old friend."

Chapter 3:

As Danny began walking back toward the stump, Lady Sue jumping from branch to branch overhead, he saw a big black crow cawing near where he had left Bernie! Bernie was in trouble!

"Hey!" Danny shouted. "You leave him alone!" Terrified, he ran back toward the stump. He shouldn't have left Bernie alone! Not even for a second! Far from his brook home, the bullfrog was in far too much danger! Danny felt like he might cry.

The crow clawed at the base of the stump. Bernie was going to be his lunch! Suddenly, from his left, Danny saw a flash of orange gray fur drop from the treetops.

It was Lady Sue! She landed right on the back of the startled crow and dug her teeth into his left-wing. The crow never saw her coming!

He let out a bloodcurdling *caw* of pain and surprise, flinging his wings up hi gh. The squirrel held on tightly, and she and the crow wrestled on the

ground as she fought to keep him away from Bernie. *She's so bra ve!* Danny thought admiringly.

The crow was more significant than she was!

He arrived at the stump to see half a dozen crow feathers lying on the ground, but finally, the crow found his footing. He hopped back up onto the stump. At last, Lady Sue lost her grip— but not without pulling out two more feathers, one in each tightly curled paw. The crow squawked down into her face and took flight.

Circling to climb into the sky, it shouted down at Danny and Lady Sue, "I'll be back, you two! And I won't be alone! You watch your back because you won't hear us coming! Caw! Caw! Caw!" The crow's injured squawks faded into the distance as he flew up and over the trees to escape.

"Whoa, that was a close one," Bernie said, crawling out from under the stump. He hopped and climbed up to the top. "Another few seconds and I would have been bullfrog à la carte!" Danny wiped his eyes.

"I'm so sorry, Bernie!" he said. "I should have watched out for that crow!" Bernie shook himself to remove the dirt from underneath the stump. "Not your fault, kid," he said unruffled. "Not your fault. I distinctly said, 'owls and hawks.' I forgot about those mangy, crafty crows.

I tell you, they're the worst because you never hear them coming. One minute, my buddy's chewing the fat next to me, then *whoosh*! He's gone! Nothing left but a sh adow riding into the sun. I've lost a lot of friends to those guys. Nasty, but I guess they have a place around here, just like the rest of us."

Bernie looked around and saw the squirrel nearby dusting herself off from the fight. He smiled wider than Danny had seen yet. “Weeeelll! How you doin’, Lady Sue?” “I’ve had better days, Bernie. I’ve had better days,” Lady Sue answered, flicking an ear with kind exasperation.

“I wanted to see you again, but not like this!” “Don’t know what I would’ve done without you, Lady Sue. Thanks.

I guess I owe you one?” “Not a chance!” Lady Sue grinned. “Don’t you remember down by the creek last year? That trout would’ve eaten
you if I hadn’t chucked that rock in its mouth. You owe me *two*, old friend!”

Bernie looked embarrassed. “Of course I remember, my dear. Wasn’t swimming too fast that day. I guess two it is.”

“I’m glad Lady Sue came to the rescue, Bernie,” Danny said. “I wouldn’t want to go on looking for a butterfly by myself.”

“So he’s looking for a butterfly?” Lady Sue said, sur- prised. “Bernie, this kid’s off his rocker! Didn’t you tell him it’s no use? No use at all!”

“I see a few early butterflies every year,” Bernie argued. “C’mon, Sue, he’s a good kid. Besides, you want to pass up a chance for a nice road trip?”

Lady Sue looked Danny up and down. "Oh, all right, all right, all right," she said. "There are no butterflies now, but it might be good to take a walk together and see what we can see."

Bernie smiled at her. "That's the spirit, old girl! Let's go for a walk and see what we can see. You can look from above, and I can look from down here. Together, we're bound to see something."

So Lady Sue ran up a tree to keep watch from above, and when Bernie was once again seated on Danny's right shoulder, the three of them set out to look for butterflies. Danny, Bernie, and Lady Sue searched for high. They searched low. But even surrounded by the magic forest, they saw no butterflies.

A few large moths caused Danny to jump with excitement before he realized—and served as an excellent snack for Bernie when they flew too close. After a while, Danny noticed he was getting hungry again. He decided to stop to have lunch. He pulled out his peanut butter sandwich and chips. He shared them with Lady Sue, who just happened to love peanuts.

But Bernie gave a disgusted, "Yuck!" He didn't want any of Danny's lunch. Instead, he looked around the base of the stump they were seated on and dug up a colony of fat, juicy grubs. "Eureka!" he cried. He ate his fill, then slowly crawled back to the group, where he settled in for a short nap.

"Bernie?" Danny whispered to his friend.

Without opening his eyes, Bernie answered. "Yeah, kid?"

“Was Lady Sue, the friend you were hoping to meet when we started?”

Bernie yawned. “Why, no, kid. Finding Sue was great, but I was thinking about someone else altogether. I wanted to meet up with Fanastacia, the fairy.”

“Fairy!” Danny exclaimed. He couldn’t believe it!

“Quiet down, kid!” Bernie chuckled. “Yeah, a fairy. *Not* like the E aster Bunny. You don’t doubt me, now, not after all you’ve seen so far?”

“Doesn’t believe in fairies!” Lady Sue laughed. “He doesn’t believe in fairies? They’re real enough out here, Danny, and they are powerful friends when you’re in need. Two winters ago, Fanastacia came to me when I didn’t have enough food for my kids and me to make it through the winter. She showed me where a squirrel that had died years before had stored a mountain of nuts! She saved us all!”

Bernie opened one lazy eye and said, “Yes, she did indeed.” Danny shook his head in wonder. “Gee, I sure hope we get to see a fairy before I have to go home.” He turned back to Lady Sue and their lunch, leaving Bernie to rest until it was time to move on.

The afternoon slipped away, and the sun slowly dipped further and further into the west—all without a sign of a single butterfly. Danny, Bernie, and Lady Sue saw a few cocoons, but t hey would not be opening for weeks to come. Danny was getting disappointed. Bernie saw how sad he was getting. He racked his brains for a new idea and eventually thought of standing watch over a beautiful wildflower. Bernie knew butterflies loved the nectar from flowers. Before too long, he spotted a flower as pretty as any he'd ever seen.

"Hey, I have an idea," he said. "Why don't we just sit here awhile with this flower and see what passes by?" Danny and Lady Sue agreed. Danny set Bernie down on the ground and watched as he hopped over to the flower and took a deep sniff of its petals. "Ah!" Bernie sighed. "That's about the sweetest flower I've ever smelled. Come on, Danny, take a whiff!"

Danny got down on his hands and knees. He put his nose right in the middle of the flower and breathed in. "Oh, yes, it's sweet enough for any butterfly!" Lady Sue sniffed the height as well. She thought she might want to chew on one of its petals. Then she saw Bernie's big eyes watching her every move. He knew the snacks she liked! This one was off-limits. "Yes, it smells delicious," she said. "I mean beautiful! It does!" Lady Sue took one more sniff, then ran up a nearby tree to look around.

Limb by limb, she climbed until she saw something hanging off a branch and swaying in the wind. It was an empty chrysalis or pupa—
one caterpillar had already changed into a butterfly! Lady Sue could not believe her eyes. She shouted down in joy, "Look up here! Look up here! See what I found! It's an empty pupa. I'm

going to chew it off and send it down to you." Lady Sue took a few bites, and the pupa slowly drifted down to Danny.

Danny looked at it in excitement. It was an empty chrysalis! "Look, Bernie! It is great! It means there are butterflies around here!" he cried. Bernie grinned. He looked up at Lady Sue. "Can you see anything else?" Lady Sue climbed higher. She looked around. "I don't see anything flying around," she reported. "It must have flown off with the—" Just then, she noticed something shimmering over in the next tree. It was a large spider web tucked deep within the branches.

The web was shaking like one of the leaves of the tree. Lady Sue went out to the very tip of the branch. To her horror, she saw a beautifully colored butterfly trapped in the web. "Oh, no! Oh no! Oh no!" she shrieked.

"There's the butterfly, trapped in that spider's web over there!" Then she saw a shadow emerging from around one of the tree branches. "Quick! Quick!" she screamed. "The spider's coming!" Horrified, Danny and Bernie watched as Lady Sue scrambled around, desperate to reach the other tree in time.

Danny began to run toward the tree with Bernie on his shoulder, holding on for dear life. Danny reached the base of the tree and, setting Bernie down, tried to climb up. But the ground was far too broad. He couldn't climb up, and Lady Sue was too far away! They couldn't reach the butterfly in time!

All of a sudden, Bernie began to croak in a high-pitched tone. It hurt Danny's ears. Danny cupped his hands over them to deaden the sound. Lady Sue stopped when she heard Bernie's piercing screech. Even the crafty spider stopped its descent down its web. But Bernie continued croaking, crying for help.

Episode 2

Chapter 1

Time seemed to stop for a moment. Then a rush of wind blew past the trio, up the tree where the butterfly was trapped. The tree leaves had hidden the spider web. Now it shimmered like a liquid net of diamonds.

Amazed, Danny saw a little light grow into the small figure of a fairy! She was dressed in beautiful colours of gold and blue. She had two sets of wings, much like those of a dragonfly. Her body was thin and athletic.

She's pretty, Danny thought*, but no human looks like that!* She wore a black helmet, much like an old-time pilot would wear. A pair of flight goggles that made them appear even bigger protected her large, beautiful eyes. It was the fairy, Fanastacia. It had to be.

Her wings beat fast, and she looked down at Bernie. The frog was now smiling wide. "I got this," Fanastacia said. She spun around and around the web. In a moment, the butterfly was no longer trapped in its sticky, silky clutches. There was no butterfly at all! It had disappeared!

The wise spider, not wishing to get involved with the fairy, climbed back up to wait for the next prey to fall into its trap. Fanastacia drifted down to Bernie and Danny, and Lady Sue climbed down to join them.

Danny blinked as Fanastacia landed softly on his left shoulder. He could scarcely breathe; he was so excited. “Hello there, young man,” Fanastacia said in a sweet, small voice. “My name is Fanastacia. I am the fairy of this forest.

I’ve heard a lot of good things about you. I’m glad to meet you finally.” “It—it’s nice to meet you,” Danny stammered, gazing at the tiny fairy pilot. “I’m sorry, Fanastacia! I didn’t believe you were real! Do you have my baby teeth?” Fanastacia laughed. “No, that’s another fairy’s job.

I’m here to help the forest remain a forest. I’m here to make sure whatever may be here remains untouched by forces from the outside world. If you didn’t want so badly to see a beautiful butterfly, I would not have come to save its day. Things would have followed their natural course.

The butterfly would have been dinner for a most deserving spider. But sometimes, I can bend the rules.” She winked at Danny. “But what happened to the butterfly?” Danny asked. Bernie and Lady Sue, standing next to one another on the ground, laughed. “Kid, take a look at your other shoulder, hey?” Bernie suggested.

Danny looked over. There it was! The beautiful butterfly was sitting on his shoulder, staring right at him! It slowly opened and closed its wings, thankfully. “Thank you,” it said. Its voice was so small! “Thank you for wishing our meeting.” It fluttered off of Danny’s shoulder. It settled onto his open palms.

Danny, careful of the butterfly's fragile wings, brought the butterfly up to his face. He stared. "You are the most beautiful butterfly I've ever seen!"

"Thank you. I can certainly say you are the most beautiful sight *I* have ever seen."

Danny walked away from the group to study his new friend. Fanastacia flew away from him to join Bernie and Lady Sue. "I'm glad you called for me, Bernardo," she said. "It's been some time since I've seen you. How are things at the brook?"

Bernie's big eyes were full of adoration. "Sometimes days are good, and sometimes not so good. It's hard to tell what humans will do when they come to visit! I've lost a lot of friends, Fanastacia, but I'm hopeful that more kids like Danny will turn things around."

"Yes, things were bad for a while," Lady Sue agreed. "But they've stopped cutting trees around here, so maybe there's a better future for our children and us."

Fanastacia smiled at them both. "I am glad times seem to be more good than bad." She looked back at Danny. "Somehow, I know this young man will play a big part in turning things around for good."

Bernie and Lady Sue looked at Danny, too. He lifted his hand and watched the butterfly fly away high into the trees. With the wind behind it, it soon drifted out of sight.

Fanastacia told everyone farewell. "You must go home now, Danny," she said. "The sun will soon be setting, and your day with us will be over. But remember this: the mysteries of the forest are here for you to forever discover and bless with your best intentions. You have made a difference already. Safe journeys for you!" With these words, Fanastacia blinked at them all. Then she vanished into thin air.

"What are you going to do about your show-and-tell, kid?" Bernie asked Danny as they made their way out of the forest with Lady Sue. Danny had told them both about his class on Monday that afternoon. "I thought the butterfly would have agreed to go with you for that."

Danny shook his head.

"I told her to go on her way," he said. "She is so beautiful here in the forest. I knew I shouldn't ask her to see my class. I'm glad she's living her life—not in a classroom or pinned in a shadow box."

Lady Sue smiled. "I'm glad I met you, Danny, but this is my stop. There's my tree. Thanks for letting me be part of the team. You're welcome to come back to visit sometime, but now you should hurry home. Your mother will be worried."

"Thank you, Lady Sue," Danny said. "Thank you for everything."

Lady Sue looked at Bernie. “So long, friend. I’ll come by soon. Soon, OK? I promise. Watch out for that nasty crow! You heard him say he’d be back!”

Bernie laughed. “I’ll keep my eyes open, Sue. Take care.”

Lady Sue scampered away, and Danny and Bernie headed back toward Bernie’s brook. As they got closer, Danny started to be sad. He knew it was almost sure he would never see his friend again. Careful of the slippery moss, he set Bernie back down by the edge of the brook. “I don’t know how to thank you, Bernie. You made my wish come true.”

Bernie blinked up at him. “No thanks needed, kid. It was a fun little trip, hey? Just remember: every living thing has a home, and everyone’s home needs to be respected. Tell those other boys that, OK? Good luck, kid. Take care of yourself and your world.” He hopped into the water.

Danny watched Bernie’s reflection under the surface of the bubbling water until it disappeared under a lily pad. Then he turned around to go home too.

Chapter 2

Monday came. All the other boys and girls came with their bullfrogs, squirrels, and baby chicks for show-and-tell. Big Bobby Collier showed up with an injured black crow in a cage. He said he had found it lying by the side of the road.

Danny Bundy had made a drawing of a beautiful butterfly. The picture was full of the colours Danny remembered from his meeting with the real one, but the colors seemed pale compared to the whole thing.

When Danny's turn came to present, he stood in front of the class. He held the picture in his hand. He told his classmates all about how he had gone into the magical forest. He explained how a beautiful butterfly had landed on his shoulder.

Also, he explained, then rested in his hand for a while. He didn't mention the talking animals or the beautiful fairy Fanastacia. He knew his classmates would laugh.

They would think he was lying. The class thought he was lying anyway. Danny's teacher, Ms. Grimes, looked up at the ceiling, impatiently waiting for him to finish. Everyone knew it was early for butterflies. After Danny finished his presentation, he received a little polite applause. But a few of his classmates laughed.

Disappointed, Danny folded up his picture. Then he felt a slight breeze coming in through the open window on his left. He turned his face into the current. He was sur- prized to see a small cloud of beautiful butterflies swirling in.

They flew all around him! Danny put his hand out, and a butterfly landed right on his palm. He recognized his friend from the forest. He smiled. He carefully raised his hand to wave it from one side of the room to the other.

All of the students' mouths dropped open. So did the teachers! After a few moments, the butterflies flew out of the window again. They floated on the wind back to their home in the forest. Danny's eyes followed his favorite butterfly all the way. Before she vanished, out of the corner of his eye, he saw a sparkling dot of light spin three times before blinking out. He gave the fairy Fanastacia a knowing smile.

Danny Bundy looked up at his teacher. "You know, Ms. Grimes, the mysteries of the forest are here for us to forever dis-cover and bless with our best intentions."

Danny won the show-and-tell contest. He made sure all the animals were taken back to their homes. Then he went to a beautiful pizza party given in his honor.

A First Plane Ride

One summer day Williams mother came outside into the back yard where he was playing. William liked the back yard because of all the trees and bushes. They made good hiding places when he pretended to be a cowboy or sheriff hunting down desperados. "William." His mother called to him.

"Come in. I have some news for you." She said. William said, "Not now mom. I am chasing the bad guys." But his mother said, "Come in. It's a surprise." When William heard that she had a surprise for him he dropped his toys and ran to her. She opened the door and William stepped into the kitchen. "What is the surprise mom?" asked William after he sat at his place at the table and picked up the peanut butter and jelly sandwich his mother had made for his lunch. "Well." his mother started to say.

"I just got off the phone with grandma in California. She wants us to go and visit her for a week. What do you think about that?"

"Wow!" said William. "Where is California?" His mother said to him, "Well, it's a long way from here. We will have to take an airplane to get there." William thought about that for a while as he took a bite of his sandwich. After some time, he looked at his mother and said, "You mean those air- planes in the sky way up in the air?" "Yes William. Way up in the air like those you see every day from the yard. "Oh boy.." said William and he got up off his chair and started to go. "Where are you going?" his mother said to him as he rushed past her. "I'm going to start packing." He said to her.

"There is still a lot of time before we have to start packing William. Why not finish your lunch and go back outside and play." She said to him. So, William finished his lunch and went out to play again but he was so excited that he didn't play cowboy any more but now he was a pilot flying a plane. When the day came William got up and dressed and his mother took him out the front door to the waiting taxi. William said to the driver, "Were going to my grandmas on an airplane."

The driver was nice and said, "That's great. Say hello to her from me." And he smiled at Williams mother. When they got to the airport William took his small suitcase and walked inside to the counter. "We're going to grandmas." He said to the lady behind the counter. "That's nice. " she answered as she handed the tickets to his mother. Then they walked out to the plane and sat there waiting for the call to board. William got up and walked to the window and looked out at the plane that was there. "Is that our airplane?" he said to his mother. "Yes William. That is the plane we are going on." After a while the agent announced that it was time to get on the plane so Williams mother took his hand

and they got on. When they found their seats, William sat by the window.

The door closed and the plans started to be pushed out." 'We are going backwards." He said. "Yes William, they have to push us out before we can take off." "What are they taking off?" asked William. "No dear. That means when we go up in the air." "Oh." Said William. When the plane was at the runway the engines started to roar and the plan moved faster and faster. William looked out of the window and his eyes were wide open as the plane moved up into the air. "Wow." Was all he could say.

His mother laughed and William held on to her hand. When the flight attendant came by later William got a glass of milk and some cookies from her. "Thank you." William said and his mother had some coffee. The flight was going to last for some hours. William never got tired looking out the window at the land below. After about an hour his eyes started to close and soon he was asleep next to his mother. A few hours later his mother woke him up. The plane had landed and the people were getting off. William stood up and he and his mother walked off and went to get their bags. When they got there William saw his grandmother waiting for them. "Grandma!" said William and she hugged and kissed him. "We rode on an airplane." He said to her. "It was super grandma." He con- tinued as they walked out to the sunny street and to her car in the parking lot. "I can hardly wait to go again." Said William as they drove out of the airport. "It was so much fun."

Leonard and the Magical Carrot

Naughty the rabbit and his friends have decided to meet at the clearing. "Hey why don't we play hide and seek?" Naughty suggests. What an excellent idea! "Everybody hide!" says Lulu the tortoise, "and I will count ... 1, 2, 3 ..."

All the animals hurry to find a good hiding place ... Naughty is looking for the perfect place to hide, but he does not realize that he has come dangerously close to the magical forest of Leonard the Wizard. A lot of strange things hap- pen here ... Actually, Naughty is not aware that he is being observed by a strange looking animal.

Before he can realize what is happening to him, Naughty feels someone catching him by his ears. "Mmh," the horrible monster says, "here is someone who seems really delicious. I am going to have a great feast." Suddenly a deep voice thunders behind him. "Let go of the rabbit immediately, Leon!" It is Leonard the Wizard who is waving his magic wand: "Abracadabra ..."

Leon, the strange dragon, gets transformed immediately into a statue and Naughty is freed from his claws. "Phew, that was scary, eh!" Leonard exclaims. "Ah, this Leon! He is always hungry! But you have to admit that it was not very intelligent of you to enter the magical forest," adds Leonard.

"Come with me," Leonard says. "I know a magic formula, which will make you invisible. So, your friends will never find you and you will win the game." As they leave poor Leon, they reassure him: "Don't worry, you will soon become normal again." When they go through the magician's vegetable plot, Naughty sees a superb carrot, which looks very bewitching and enticing.

Naughty is unable to control himself and sinks his teeth into the carrot ... "Oh no, don't do that!" Leonard cries out. Too late ... Naughty has already been transformed into a small white hen! "You shouldn't have touched that carrot," moans the magician.

"I should never have brought you here," Leonard says. "You rabbits always eat my carrots; so I had to cast a spell, which transforms you into a hen. Because as you know Naughty, hens don't like carrots." "But I don't want to be a hen!" Naughty exclaims. "Well, all this is very annoying," grumbles Leonard. "OK, I'll let you off this time. I will see if I can find something in my magic book of spells that will give you your rabbit shape back. Come with me, we will certainly find a solution."

Once they reach the magician's house, Leonard opens the door and invites the hen to come in. "Ah, here it is, my magic book of spells," Leonard says, "let's see if I can find the right formula and then, within a few seconds, this whole thing will just be a bad memory."

While Leonard the Wizard is consulting his precious book, the bell rings. Ding dong. "Ah, we have a visitor. Who could it possibly be?" Leonard opens the door and discovers Lulu the tortoise in a dreadful state.

"Ah! Dear magician sir," she says. "Have you by any chance seen Naughty the rabbit? We were playing hide and seek and we can't find him anywhere. And what if he has been gobbled up by Leon the dragon?"

"Not at all," Leonard answers. "Leon did not eat your friend up. Come on in, let me introduce you to Naughty the hen." "Naughty the hen?" says Lulu, all surprised. But when she recognizes her friend, she bursts out laughing.

"Oh Naughty, how funny! You have been turned into a hen!" she says in a fit of laughter. "So what? I don't see what's so funny about it!" Naughty protests. Meanwhile, Leonard flicks through his magic book of spells. "Ah, yippee! I have found the magic spell," he exclaims. "Abracadabra!" And in a flash, Naughty the hen turns back into Naughty the rabbit again.

Naughty is relieved. He definitely prefers his soft white fur to the hen's feathers. Naughty promises Leonard that he will never bite his carrots again and the two friends take leave of the magician. “You know Lulu,” says Naughty, “it was not very nice being a hen. I feel much better as a little rabbit.”

Flying a Kite

William's father had weekends off from work. One such Saturday morning William's father sat down to eat breakfast as William was there eating some cereal. "William, how about we do something today?" his father said to him. William looked at his father and said, "What can we do daddy?" William's father squinted his eyes at him and said, "What do you think we can do?" William thought a little then raised his shoulders. "I don't know." He said. "I think I know what we can do. Why don't we go buy a kite and fly it in the back yard?" said his father. "Yippee." Cried William. "Can we go now daddy?" he said getting out of his chair and coming around to his father's side.

"Let me finish here and then we can go." William put his dish into the sink where his mother was standing and ran to his room. He pulled out a jacket from the closet and ran back to the kitchen where his father was just about done eating. When they were ready William and his father got into the car and drove to the store. When the got there William ran to the display where the kites were and started to pick out the one that he liked. When his father came over he said, "Is that the one?" and William said, "Yes, this is the one I want daddy." William couldn't wait to get home. When they got there William rushed into the house to show the kite to his mother. "Look at this kite mommy. It's pretty don't you think so?" "Why yes William. It's very nice." She said to him. When his father came in they went outside into the back yard with the kite and a big roll of string.

William's father tied the kite to the end of the string and told William to go to the other end of the yard with the kite. So William took the kite and ran to the far end of the yard. When he let go the kite took off. The wind was just right. "Wow." Said William. "Here William. " His father said as he gave William the end of the string. William held on tight as the kite moved left and right with the wind. "This is fun." Said William. That night William dreamed of the kite and how it took him up into the air. It was a very good dream for William.

www.ingramcontent.com/pod-product-compliance
Lightning Source LLC
Chambersburg PA
CBHW070627310726
48982CB00001B/195

* 9 7 8 1 9 1 4 2 3 2 4 3 5 *